My Kismot's Beloveds

Kimberly M. Ringer

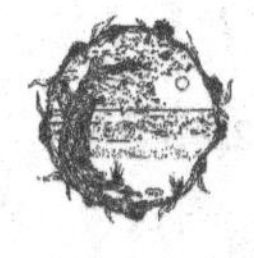

Kimberly M. Ringer

Contact Information: www.kimberlymringer.com

Header photo obtained from CreativeFabrica.com

Print ISBN: 978-1-957447-24-7

E-Book ISBN: 978-1-957447-23-0

First Edition: November 2023

Tara, Sarren, Elisabeth, and Mama Hen (Cindy),

You wanted his story, because I couldn't leave him
the only unmated one of the three.
He thanks you very much for the nudging that you
provided.

Love you with all my arse and anxiety.
-Kim-

Content Considerations

Pregnancy
Infertility
Pregnancy Complications
Surgery
Discussions of Self Identity
MMF
LGBTQIA+
Explicit Sexual content
Death

This list is not meant to be complete and all encompassing. Please be mindful of your mental health.

If you or someone you know may be struggling with suicidal thoughts, you can call the U.S. National Suicide Prevention Lifeline by simply dialing 988 or the full phone number 800-273-TALK (8255) any time, day or night, or chat online. Crisis Text Line also provides free, 24/7, confidential support via text message to people in crisis when they dial 741741.

DEDICATION

To anyone who has waited for love and find it at the most unusal times.

CONTENTS

ASHSTRIKE SANCTORUM

THE OVERSEEING PRIMALS

MINSTREL
ALWAYS AN ASTRAL & SEER
ONE OTHER TO BE DETERMINED

ASTRAL PRIMAL   EXORCI PRIMAL

ASTRALS AND EXORCI'S

SPECIES PRIMALS

SPECIES HEADS

KISMOT	THERUGI
WEREWOLF	IMMORTALS
BACRI	SEERS
AAMANTI	PHRENIC
CHANGLING	OVEXA
IAMU	ANGELS
PUROKLETS	WITCHES
KIR	VAMPIRES
CALASSEI	FAE

Ashstrike Sanctorum Creature Registry

Astral:	Encforcer / Emissary with Daggers
Angels:	Winged creatures
Changling:	Humanoid shapeshifte
Exorci:	Executioners
Fae:	elusive, secretive, not much is known
Immortals:	Humans turned Immortal by the dark moesia witches
Ovexa:	super talented tracke and used as investigators
Phrenic:	Physic / Mind control
Seers:	See the future

THERUGI:	DEMON CLASSIFICATION CATCH ALL
VAMPIRES:	DRINK BLOOD FOR SUBSTANCE
WITCHES:	USUALLY TALENTED IN HEALING POWERS, SOME VARIATIONS

ELEMENTALS

CALASSEI:	CONTROLS AIR
IAMU:	CONTROLS FIRE
KIR:	CONTROLS EARTH
PUROKLET:	CONTROLS WATER

SHIFTERS

AAMANTI:	DRAGON
BACRI:	EAGLE / OTHER BIRDS
KISMOT:	MOUNTAIN LION
WEREWOLF:	WOLF

CHAPTER 1

HADRIAN

After meeting with Doc, we decided it was best to head straight over to Princess Ronni and introduce ourselves. Doc had mentioned that they had already spoken with one of Prince Masen's hands and advised him we would be taking over for Doc while they recovered from a serious case of pneumonia. Doc had explained that the princess had a difficult time conceiving due to major trauma over the years, and when news had spread of her being pregnant with twins, apparently the whole pride had thrown a celebration.

Removing the face shield and the paper gown I had worn while we were in with Doc, I tossed them and the nitrile gloves into the trash. While my queen mate, Marie, stood there looking out the window, I couldn't help but smile at her. Three and a half years ago, I had walked into a bar in Reno, Nevada, and saw her dancing with some of her friends. They had just finished passing their final boards and were having a celebratory weekend out of town. With one look, she knocked me on my proverbial ass.

I never thought I would find a mate, let alone a queen mate. I'd always leaned toward men, but when our eyes locked and my inner tom roared she was mine, I didn't handle it well. To say I had an identity crisis was putting it mildly. She stood by me the entire time, though, and reassured me she wouldn't hold me back from enjoying men. She wouldn't change who I was, but she reminded me that she was mine and I was hers. It took six months of me working on being confident enough to accept who I was and seeing that she really was there for me before I agreed to mate her. Not because I doubted her, but because I doubted myself. The fact was, I didn't feel worthy of the queen she was. Sure, our cats loved each other. It just took some time for my human side to come to grips with it.

Now, looking at her with her long red hair half up, the rest flowing down her back, and those full curves, I didn't know what I would do without her. She had Princess Ronni's chart in front of her on the table, but she wasn't paying any attention to it. She'd been playing with the stethoscope, just rolling it in her hands while staring out the window.

"Ready to see how Princess Ronni is doing?" I whispered in her ear. She nodded but still seemed distracted. I wrapped an arm around her waist, took the stethoscope from her hand, and set it next to the princess's chart before turning her and pulling her close. "What's wrong?"

Marie lifted her hand and trailed her fingers against the mating mark, just where the shoulder met my neck. "I'm getting *that* feeling again."

Understanding filled me. About two years ago, she had come to me and said that she knew we were mates, but she felt like something was missing. I had asked if she wanted cubs, but she just shrugged. Marie wasn't against having kids, but she didn't feel like that was what was missing at the time. It took a while, but while we realized that we both had found a part of ourselves when we mated, we somehow knew it wasn't going to be just the two of us.

"Do you think we will find them here?"

"I don't know," she murmured as she leaned forward and rested her forehead on my chest.

I was a full head taller than her, and I loved how she just fit against me. With a kiss to the top of her head, I said, "Well, let's go check on the princess, and then we can walk Landow. Let's see if anyone catches those beautiful green eyes."

Lifting her head, she shook it. "I'm more worried about you."

I feigned shock. "Why? I don't know what you mean."

Marie rolled her eyes and just said, "For a thirty-three-year-old tom, I worried that you would lose interest in sex, but fuck if my mate doesn't jump at any chance to please."

When her eyes heated, I smelled her arousal, and my tom let out a growl. "Baby, I swear. If we didn't have a patient waiting for us, I would take you back to the cabin and show you *just* how much you don't have to worry about my testosterone levels."

"That's right, Nurse Fuller. Be professional," she teased, retreating from my arms.

This time, it was me who rolled my eyes. "Like Dr. Fuller didn't start it."

CHAPTER 2

LEO

"Doc says bed rest until we can schedule a cesarean," I told her, arms crossed tight across my chest.

Ronni's eyes went wide. "I'm sorry, what? I don't think so."

"Kitten, think about it—"

She cut Masen off with a harsh glare. "I've been on modified bed rest for two months!" Ronni's lips were pinched so tight, they were almost white.

"Ronni, the twins need to cook a little longer," I said carefully.

"And you were the poor soul that was tasked with delivering the message. Why isn't Doc here telling me?"

I shifted on my feet, running my hands through my hair. "Ahh, well, as you know, they kind of came down with pneumonia. It's really bad. They don't want to chance getting you sick this close to the twins being born. So, they have an associate of theirs coming down to fill in for a bit. Doc is going to quarantine until they are feeling better."

"They have someone coming from out of town? Why isn't the physician's assistant, Jarrett, just covering it?" Masen said, holding his mate's hand. My best friend and Crown Prince to the Ventana Wilderness Pride looked nervous as hell.

"I'm starting to wonder, Mase, who is more nervous about this pregnancy, you or Ronni?" I chuckled.

Ronni turned to face her husband, smiled, and ran a hand over her large belly. "He's just worried. With all the issues, even conceiving, and all . . ."

I smiled at the love that shone in their eyes as they looked at each other. Ronni had been through so much before she was forced to marry Masen, only to learn that she was his gods given mate three years ago.

"Jarrett is good, but the doctor coming in specializes in high-risk pregnancies. Doc said that the doctor and nurse were stopping by their place this morning to check in on them and to get the rundown on your pregnancy and medical history."

There was a knock on the doorframe, and then Morgan's head popped through the doorway. "Um, speaking of the doc and nurse, they are here to see Ronni. You good?"

"Good timing," Masen said at the same time I complained, "Anything to take the pressure off me. Apparently, I'm the evil one just for relaying information from Doc."

Morgan turned to where I assumed the doctor and the nurse were standing and waved them in before coming into the bedroom and standing on the other side of the bed.

Just as the duo walked in the door, my entire body came alive. A tall, dark tom stepped in first, and when light-blue eyes met mine, heat burst through me. Before I could blink, he had me pushed against the wall and purred, "Mine."

My tom was going wild as the world spun, and I smiled, grabbing him by the waist, dislodging his hold on me as I reversed our positions. I leaned in toward him and growled, "Mine."

"Fucking hell," he purred as his hands slid down my waist and gripped my shirt.

A finger hooked my chin, pulled it toward the face of an angel, and it was as if the shuffled cards of my life fell into a neat stack. My chest thumped twice, and I swore I saw theirs do the same. The breath left my lungs, but I quickly recovered as my tom roared in satisfaction. "Also mine."

My focus bounced between the two of them, and I slowly released my hold on the stunning tom before me. My heart was racing.

Two mates. I have two mates. A tom and a queen.

"Fucking finally." I heard Morgan and Masen say behind me, where there was a loud clap and chuckling.

Finally was right.

I took a step back, but the male didn't remove his hand from where it rested on my hip, and the queen had reached down to thread her fingers with mine. My gaze took in her stunning green eyes, fiery red hair, and soft curves I couldn't wait to get my hands on. My attention narrowed on her shoulder, where a small white scar sat. Looking at the same spot on the man, whose hand had tightened on my waist, I tried not to feel jealous that they had already gone so far without me. "You've already mated?"

"We have. A few years ago, but we both always felt like something was missing. Like there was a piece of us out there, still floating around. I'm Hadrian Fuller, by the way."

"Leo Banks." I swallowed and looked over at her and asked, "And my queen mate?"

Red lined her cheeks. "Marie."

"Hadrian and Marie. My mates." I swallowed again. My heart was still beating hard against my chest as I just stood there, taking them in. He was about my height, and his hair was cut close to his head but longer on top.

Good enough to hold on to.

I felt all that tingly warmth spread through me and my shoulders loosened. Ronni, however, took that moment to be a smart ass. "Oh, so I get doctor-ordered bed rest while Leo gets to go play with two mates? Mase, how in the hell is that fair?"

Chuckling as Marie and Hadrian stood there and blinked in confusion, I turned and waved my hand in the air, saying, "Yeah, well, you playing with your mate got you into this position."

"Yeah, okay, *Uncle Leo*. It isn't like you weren't just as happy about the pregnancy as the rest of us."

"Totally not the point." Rolling my eyes, I faced my mates again and smiled. Reluctantly, I turned but sandwiched myself between the two of them to face Ronnie and my brothers. "Marie, Hadrian, the smart ass in the bed is Princess Ronni. The shitheads next to her, Prince Masen being one of them, are my brothers. Right now, I'm liking the one *not* clutching onto Ronni a bit more. His name is Morgan."

Hadrian chuckled next to me, and it warmed my soul. It was Marie, though, who stepped up, regaining her composure, and said, "It's nice to meet you. I am Dr. Marie Fuller. I'll be stepping in for Doc to see you through the next month of your pregnancy." She looked back at me and smiled brightly. "But it looks like we will be getting to know each other much more and I might, if given the chance, get to be a part of those babes' lives."

Ronni laughed, ran her hands over her large, round stomach, and looked down just as the babes started moving around. She winced and narrowed her eyes at them. "I was trying to introduce you to your new aunt and uncle. Did you have to kick my ribs in response?"

Hadrian's hand tightened on my hip, and he let it slowly fall from me as he took a step forward, next to Marie. "It's nice to meet you, Princess Ronni."

Then, that woman raised an eyebrow and said, "Oh no. If you are mated to Leo, you are family, so no formalities."

"I'm sorry, princess, but while in the capacity of your physicians, you are the Princess of the Ventana Wilderness Pride and you will be treated as such," Hadrian said firmly.

Marie's attention went to me, and I shrugged. She raised her eyebrows and turned back around, chuckling. "Well, I was sent here to check on you, princess."

When Ronni went to say something, Marie crossed her arms over her chest and jutted a hip out. I bit my lip and had this undeniable urge to reach over and pull her close to me. Hadrian gave me a sexy sideways glance that said, *I know, right?*

I gave him a quick acknowledgement nod and realized I needed just a moment to gather my thoughts. Water. I could get Ronni some water while my mates did their jobs.

My mates.

My attention bounced between the two of them as they were talking to Ronni and Masen. When I took a deep breath through my nose, their scents permeated my senses—whiskey and maple syrup. I stepped around Hadrian to grab the empty cup on her bedside table. "Looks like you are out of water, Ronni. I'll get more. Give you and Marie a moment."

Morgan stepped out of the room with me, and when we got into the kitchen, I leaned on the counter and tried to remember how to breathe.

Morgan's hand landed on my shoulder and squeezed. "Told you that you would find them some day."

A ball of emotion filled my throat, and I felt the tears gathering in my eyes. "A tom and a queen," I whispered.

"Everything you've ever wanted, brother." His voice was soft, and I took a deep breath as his focus went behind us. There was a quick nod, and then he said, "Now, if you don't mind, I'm going to go tell Angelica she has a new brother and sister."

"We haven't mated yet." I huffed a laugh.

"Yet." Then, he was gone.

Standing there, looking out the window over the sink, I let the reality of the situation wash over me. A ragged breath rattled my chest as I let the tears of joy fall. When my breathing hitched on the next breath, strong arms wrapped around my waist and a small kiss was pressed against my shoulder. The smell of a sweet whiskey circled me, and I couldn't help but let out a relieved breath.

"I'm sorry it took us so long to find you, Leo." I swallowed and turned to face him. Hadrian's eyes met mine, and he reached up and wiped away the tears. "I'm so sorry."

I leaned into his touch. It was warm, comforting, and my chest tightened again as I swallowed. "This isn't your fault."

"I know, but . . ." He took a deep breath.

I held his gaze, watching the devotion and heat rise in it. It snapped something inside me. I moved so his back was pressed against the cabinets, and when his moan rippled through me, it had me instantly hardening for him. He bit his bottom lip as he said, "Fuck."

My eyebrow twitched, but then my gaze went to his lips. Running my hand up his chest, I wrapped it around the side of his throat, and his whole body loosened against me. "Can I kiss you, Hadrian?"

"Please."

Leaning forward, I breathed against his lips. "Thank the gods."

The kiss started soft, his long scruff tickling my skin, sending goose bumps shooting down my neck. My tongue swept over his lips, rich whiskey enveloping my senses as he opened for me. Every ounce of me needed this man. My hips pressed against his, and I felt his hardness against mine. Hadrian moaned into me, and I rolled against him.

Fuck, the man could kiss. His hands wrapped around me and slid down to grab my ass as my fingers tightened on his neck, enticing another moan from him. When my lungs were screaming for air, I pulled back, kissing him softly again.

His eyes opened and as his focus cleared, he smiled. "Damn."

Smirking and letting a little of that mischief light my eyes, I stepped back. My head tilted to the side as I heard Ronni answering Marie's questions. I kissed Hadrian quickly again and let out a quick breath before I grabbed Ronni's tumbler, added some ice, filled it with water, and then reached out for his hand. When he took it, a flood of calmness filled me. I let out a relieved breath as we headed back to the bedroom, where Marie turned and saw us holding hands. A bright smile crossed her face. "There are my boys."

Hadrian's hand squeezed mine quickly before he let go, stepped forward, and reached for the paperwork and a pen. "Notes?"

She nodded and then started dictating a bunch of instructions that all seemed like half words and gibberish to me. I brought Ronni her water, and when I handed it to her, there was a glint in her eye.

"Shush."

"What? I can't be happy for you?"

I gave her an even look. "Just because I found them doesn't mean that my loyalties to you and Masen go anywhere. I still have a duty to protect my pride's prince and princess."

Her attention didn't leave mine as my mates inspected her stomach. "But it will shift, which it should. Masen is the pride prince, but he still found a way to balance me and his duty. You will need to do the same."

I could feel Marie's and Hadrian's gazes on me, and I let out a long breath. I couldn't look at them before I said it, so I focused hard on Ronni. "First, we need to sort out their responsibilities and mine, and then I need to find out if they will even stay in Landow."

"Excuse me!" Marie exclaimed. "And why in the hell do you think we *wouldn't* be staying?"

Swallowing, I turned to them and lifted my chin. "I am honor bound to Prince Masen." They didn't look at each other, but their expressions were mirrored as they silently said, *Obviously*. "Okay, things to talk about."

"Let's finish up here, and then maybe we can go for coffee and talk about this," Marie said carefully. Swallowing, I nodded and looked back to Ronni, who was smiling at me with that look that told me to work it out.

CHAPTER 3

MARIE

It was almost impossible to focus on Princess Ronni after Leo, *my mate . . . our mate,* walked out of the room, but I was a professional and shoved it aside to be the competent doctor Doc knew and trusted me to be. When Hadrian and I walked into the bedroom, my queen straight roared in victory at the sight of Leo standing there. If Hadrian hadn't rushed for him, I would have. The only thing keeping me from joining him was the fact Hadrian, despite his statements that he didn't care if they were male or female, needed Leo. He needed a tom in our family.

I didn't care one way or the other. We had been with both females and males, but I hadn't failed to notice how much more satisfied Hadrian had been when it was a male. So yes, Leo was exactly what our family needed.

When Hadrian couldn't stop glancing at the door after Morgan returned, I sent him out under the guise of checking on the princess's water.

"That was really sweet of you," Prince Masen said.

Making a few notes, I asked, "What was?"

"The way you let him go out to be with Leo." I lifted my gaze from the chart and met his eyes. "The three of us all found our mates late. Leo, I think, had given up hope he would find you. Well, I guess find the both of you."

"Will he be okay with Hadrian?" I asked softly, worried that Leo may not want to have a relationship with a tom, when I knew just how much Hadrian did.

"Of course, and not just because he's his mate. Leo has never cared about the gender of the person, just the quality of them. If I know my brother for anything, he's going to jump in with both feet with you two. Please don't hurt him."

"Never." My queen growled at the thought of Leo being in pain. "I can't wait to get to know the person he is. My queen is being pretty rude right now, but she's gonna have to wait." She huffed at me and curled up in the back corner of my mind. "Besides, we need to see how these babes are doing."

Hadrian didn't immediately return, and it allowed my mind to wander a bit as I systematically went through my checklist. Ronni answered all my questions, saying that for the most part, she felt fine, just didn't really appreciate having to go on full-time bed rest.

"Princess Ronni, you know how high-risk the pregnancy is. I'm sure Doc has given you every statistic out there to make you understand—"

"Oh, I understand the science behind why my ass rarely needs to leave this bed and why I'm not allowed to shift anymore. I just don't like it."

There was a soft thump from the other room, and my hearing picked up on the delightful sound of Hadrian's moan. *Good.*

I took a deep breath and continued on, both amused and jealous of what was happening between my mates. When he walked in, hand in hand with Leo, the smell of their mutual arousal wrapped around me. I had to close my eyes and take a settling breath so that I could finish up. It also didn't fail my notice that the prince and princess gave each other knowing looks.

After ensuring the prince and princess that their babies were healthy, that Ronni's health was good all things considered, and addressed Leo's verbalized concerns, they both practically kicked us out of the room.

"Go spend time with Leo." There were tears in her eyes and a wide smile on her face. "He's not the only one who's been waiting."

With a final nod, I headed from the room and sought out my mate . . . No, my *mates*. My heart swelled at the thought, and I hurried my steps. After rounding a corner into the living room, I ran into a very muscular chest and smiled when I recognized not one, but two scents.

"Marie." Leo's quiet, gravelly voice, heavy with desire, sent goose bumps rippling down my back.

I looked up and into his blue eyes. "There you are. I was hoping I wouldn't have to go far to find you again."

A sad smile twitched at the corner of my mouth. "You'll never have to go far to find me. I'll always be here for you."

Hadrian's low growl rumbled. "And we're going to be here for you, too."

I took a deep breath, already loving how Hadrian and Leo's scents combined: whiskey and apples. "Would you like to take this conversation back to our cabin? I had to be professional with the prince and princess, but there's nothing I want to do right now that would be professional *or* appropriate for public consumption."

Desire flared in both men's eyes, but it was Hadrian who made the first move. Grabbing the bag slung over my shoulder with our things in it, he took both of our hands in his and practically dragged us out of the house.

Leo, however, pulled us to a stop. "Wait, where were you assigned?"

"Down a couple blocks," I told him, but there was a large smile on his face when he shook his head.

"Not anymore. This way." He turned, and we went down about half a block before we were standing on the porch of another home. Leo swung the door open and held his hand out.

I held his hand tight as Hadrian went in first. When I didn't immediately move, Leo pulled me through the door, and once we were all inside, he shut it. "Welcome home."

Home.

Looking around the living room, I could see it was simple, yet efficient. Every piece had a function other than looks. Even the ottoman was a storage unit. It was much like Prince Masen's, but the furniture was a lighter brown. Walking around the room, I went to the far wall and saw dozens of framed photos of Prince Masen and Morgan with Leo.

Leo's arms encircled me, and when I looked over my shoulder, I kissed his jaw as Hadrian wrapped his arm around Leo. "You've known them for a long time."

"When I said they were my brothers, I meant it. We've known each other since we were toddlers. The king and queen took me in when my parents died in an accident when I was a kid. The three of us are trouble, and if you stick around, you'll see that."

I huffed angrily through my nose, and this time I wasn't going to take it. "That is twice now you've assumed we are leaving." Stepping out of his embrace, I whirled around. With my finger outstretched, I laid into him. "You are our mate. Mates don't abandon each other. Do I have a practice and a life in Eureka? Sure, but that doesn't mean shit. We will happily give it all up to be with you."

The pain that tightened around his eyes pierced me in the heart. His breath was shallow as he asked, "Why? I couldn't ask you to do that."

Hadrian echoed what I just said. "Did you not hear our queen? We are mates, love." His hand reached out and cradled my cheek. "Marie and I have discussed it before. When we realized there was someone else out there for us, moving or relocating was something we knew we would have to come to an agreement on."

"Hadrian and I decided that if our mate had responsibilities that wouldn't allow them to relocate, then we would. We never thought you'd be the hand to the prince of the most powerful Kismot pride in North America, but I mean, that would qualify as being in a position that wouldn't be easy to leave."

When Leo looked back at me, I raised my eyebrows at him. "Well, are you going to continue to fight us on it, or do I finally get to have a taste of you? Not going to lie. I'm a little jealous Hadrian has already." He blinked at me, studying me closely. "Kiss me, Leo."

A smirk lifted the side of his mouth as he took a step toward me and cradled my face in his warm, calloused hands. "So demanding."

"Sometimes," I purred, just before his lips met mine, warm and sweet. Grasping onto his belt, I pulled him close and opened for him. His tongue explored every inch of my mouth, and with every swipe, heat spread through me, and I could feel him hardening against me.

I had just slid my hands up the front of his shirt when he leaned back and sighed. "I'm sorry to info-dump on you."

"Love, we all have a history," Hadrian murmured, and Leo looked at him. "We both know what it is like not to have family around us. To make our own way." Looking between us, he waited. "My parents are still in Nevada and run with a small pride up there. They own a construction company for the locals. Both human and Kismot alike. They aren't so bad. It's the extended family that's bullshit."

Looking down at Leo's chest, I muttered, "I'll explain more later, but my parents died when I was a teen. My best friend's parents let me stay with them afterwards. It's a typical doctor's story really." I let out a long breath as I pushed the memories back. "I never really knew any of my extended family, so I created my own. When my best friend mated, I was happy for her, but her mate was from Indiana, so she moved and finished her education out there. I still go to see her on occasion, but the wolves get twitchy around me, so we usually just meet in Indy."

"Your best friend is a wolf?"

Shaking my head, I replied, "Human actually." I smiled and even Hadrian laughed. "Shocked the hell out of her mate, but she's happy."

Leo looked to Hadrian, who swallowed before saying, "I had friends in Reno when I met Marie, but . . . when I found her, they—"

"Were dicks," I blurted.

"They were complete dicks. While I was coming to grips with finding her, I would not tolerate them treating Marie, my mate, less than we were. It was, unfortunately, the way my pride worked. The women were deemed less than the men. I never understood it." His hand reached out and cupped my cheek. "I always thought our queens should be worshiped and our number one priority, but . . ." He shook his head. "It wasn't a hardship to move with her to Eureka."

Slowly, I lifted my head up to see Leo looking between us, and I could see the wheels turning in his head. I was about to ask about it, but a knock sounded through the room. His growl was low as he pulled away, kissed me softly again, and then turned for the door.

When he opened it, one of the king's guards was standing there. "King Harsu requires your presence."

"Masen and Morgan as well?" The guard nodded in confirmation, and Leo said, "Throne or conference room?"

"Conference."

There was a muttered, "*Fuck*," before he continued, "Noted. Thank you. Are you notifying the prince and Morgan?" His gaze flicked to where we were standing before going back to the guard.

"No, sir. I was sent to retrieve you only."

"Very well. I want you to help Dr. Fuller and Hadrian move their belongings here. Is that understood?"

Warmth filled me, but I burst out, "I'm sorry, what?"

He turned and came to stand before us. "I believe you heard what I asked the guard to do."

"I did, but—"

"No buts. However, I will ask you properly. Will my mates do me the honor of moving into our home?"

Feeling cocky, I smiled at him and teased, "You seem pretty sure of yourself."

Smirking, he bent down and kissed me softly before whispering against my lips, "Didn't my mates lay into me earlier that they were going to stay here? Or did I mishear that whole dressing down you gave me?"

Hadrian chuckled next to me, and the sound made my whole body heat. Fuck, these two were going to be the death of me. "We'll move our stuff."

"Good. Bedroom is at the far end of the hall. I'll be home as soon as I can." Then, he leaned over and gave Hadrian a quick kiss before striding out the door.

The guard smiled, tipped his head, and simply said, "Welcome home. I'll be outside when you are ready to leave."

After he slowly shut the door, I looked at Hadrian, who was blushing. "Baby, we hit the fucking jackpot."

"Yeah, we did."

Wrapping an arm around his waist, I leaned against him. Looking around our new home, I couldn't help but think that everything was simple but had a very calming feel to it. "I like it here."

With a kiss to the top of my head, Hadrian headed down the hall while I went to the kitchen to see if there was anything to cook for dinner. Opening the fridge, I saw a couple steaks and a few odds and ends, but it was clear he didn't have enough to cover all three of us. I knew how much Hadrian needed to eat to keep up his strength, and so I made a mental note to stop by the little store and set up an account for groceries.

"Baby . . . ," Hadrian called, and I hurried down the hall where he was standing. "Ummm . . . room to sleep won't be a problem."

CHAPTER 4
HADRIAN

Standing next to Marie, I looked around the room. It was perfect. There, along the single dark-blue wall, was the only piece of furniture in the room, an Alaskan King bed. I made my way over to the edge and ran my hand along the duvet and to the headboard. It was dark blue and had thin paw patterns in grey. A single window was on the wall to the right, with two doors to the left. Turning to open the first one, I was presented with a giant walk-in closet. Only a small section of it had some jeans, various T-shirts, and about six long-sleeve dress shirts, with dress pants hung neatly in a row next to them. As I ran my fingers across them, Marie stood in the doorway, looking around in awe.

My focus went to a bright-blue, long-sleeve button-up, and as I fingered the cuff, I pictured him standing over me in nothing but this shirt.

"What are you thinking about that brought that smile to your face?"

My whispered response was barely audible even to my own ears. "I want him in this and nothing else." Smiling, I turned to face her. "Did he know he would have two mates?" I let out a breath. "He genuinely seemed surprised when he looked at both of us and realized we were his."

Her brain was working a million miles a minute. "How are you feeling?"

"Don't question my love for you. I love you with everything I am."

"That isn't what I asked and you know it. I have never doubted your love for me, Hadrian. How do you feel here?" She put her hand over my heart and ran her thumb back and forth.

Realization at what she was really asking had me running my hand through my hair and taking a deep, easy breath. I checked in with my tom, and he was quietly purring and content. "It's strange to say, but like I can breathe."

"Me too."

Meeting her gaze, I took her hand and asked, "You okay? I know we've been with both, but is there a problem with him being male?"

"Gods, no, Hadrian." She stepped back and laughed. "I was more concerned that he would have a problem with you, but the prince assured me that wouldn't be an issue."

I could feel the rise of heat in my cheeks. "That kiss in the kitchen and the feel of his cock against mine earlier prove that statement." Marie shook her head, and I just shrugged. "Hey, you can't deny that you've already thought about what it would be like on your knees before him on that bed."

"Not denying it one damn bit." Her smile was bright as she took a deep breath. "Let's go to the store and get something to make our mate for dinner when he gets home. Then, we will go grab the suitcases and just set them here."

As we walked out the door, the guard stood straighter. "What can I do for you, Dr. Fuller?"

"Ummm . . ." She looked at him and just said, "Well, I need to stop by the grocery store and see if they can set up an account—"

"Simply ask them to put them on Leo's tab. He'll take care of it."

Marie was quick to say, "No. I can pay for my own food."

"It's not . . . Oh, well, I'm sorry. I must have misinterpreted earlier. My apologies."

Intrigued, I tipped my head to the side. "What did you misinterpret?"

"I assumed that since he kissed you both goodbye and asked you to move in, that he had found his mates?" His focus bounced between us, and I smiled.

"He has, but that doesn't mean we can't pay for our own food."

The guard, while looking relieved that he hadn't been wrong, was still surprised. "The hand of the crown prince will not allow his mates to pay for anything for him. You are welcome to try, though. Since you are mates, you might have a chance at changing the mind of a man who is used to having his orders followed." He stepped off the porch and waited for us to join him. "The store first, then we will get your things from the cabin."

Just as the guard had said, Justine, the older kismot who ran the general store, insisted that while he would set up an account for us, he wouldn't put anything on it. The guard hadn't said who we were to him, but had merely informed that we were staying with Leo for now.

"Leo would have my hide if I let his guests pay for food." Justine genuinely looked like he was offended I would even ask such a thing.

Bags of groceries in hand, we stopped by the house to put them away, only to find that our suitcases and the extra duffle bag were sitting in the living room at the front of the hallway. How in the hell did they get here? Did Leo send for them? We said we would go get our stuff.

After unloading the groceries, I started helping Marie prepare dinner. We searched the kitchen for what we needed and were glad to see he had it well stocked with kitchen supplies. I loved to bake, so I looked forward to being able to get to work on the weekends. Fresh bread, cinnamon rolls, pastries, cakes, and so much more.

She was staring at the ingredients for her taco lasagna when my tom started stirring and I felt her panic through the bond. "Baby, what's wrong?"

"What if he's allergic to tomatoes? What if he can't have dairy?" Her eyes were wide, and I put my hands on the side of her face, making her focus on me.

"Breathe, baby. Breathe."

She took a deep breath, and I breathed with her. After a few more, I pulled her in tight to my chest, holding her until she had calmed.

"I love the fact your scents go together so well. It's a sweet apple whiskey."

"Yeah, well, your maple goes pretty damn well with it, too. Adds to the sweetness. We complement each other, baby."

Nodding, she pulled back and said, "So make the meal?"

"Make the damn meal, beautiful."

I opened the jars and laid out everything for her to layer the dish. Stepping back, I watched as my queen went about making dinner.

She was nearly done when the crisp scent of a sweet apple became stronger in the room. A moment later, there was a soft kiss on my cheek, and I turned to face him. "Welcome home."

He smiled and walked over to where Marie was, wrapping his arms around her waist, murmuring, "You're making dinner?"

CHAPTER 5
MARIE

"**I** am."

"You don't have to cook for me. I was planning on making dinner for you. Had just stopped by here first because I needed to make sure you weren't a fever dream." His nose nestled into my neck and he took a deep inhale, hummed, and whispered, "Warm maple syrup."

"We were just talking about that. I love how the two of you create a sweet apple whiskey."

"Where I get maple whiskey." He placed a small kiss right next to Hadrian's mating mark and ran his tongue along it. My knees gave out, and he chuckled. "Easy."

"That's not fair," I whispered. "Now, go get cleaned up."

When he stepped back, I put dinner in the oven and turned to see him staring at the suitcases, eyebrows knitting together.

Hadrian went to stand next to him, and I went to his other side and took Leo's hand. "I-I know I asked, but really more like demanded and then had your things moved over. I'm sorry if I overstepped. As hand to the crown prince, I'm used to having my orders followed, except when it comes to Masen, Ronni, and Morgan. Yeah, okay, so Morgan's wife, Angelica, usually listens, but . . ."

"Your rambling is adorable," Hadrian said, but I pulled Leo around to face me.

"Do I have to be the one in this relationship to keep your head on straight? I mean, we've only known each other for not even a day, but at what point did I give off the impression I'm going to allow anyone to toss me around?"

Hadrian snicked, and I gave him an even look, because I knew he had pictured how he had tossed me on the bed and held me down while he did any number of amazing things to my body.

When my attention went back to Leo, there was a sliver of playfulness in his eyes. "I'm a doctor, Leo. I've had to assert myself as a female in a male field. Now, what is it you really want to know?"

Leo's shoulders tightened slightly, and he looked away for a moment. I swore it looked as if he was protecting himself from my response. He reached up and tucked a string of my hair behind my ear. I didn't expect the slight tremble to his touch. "You haven't unpacked."

"Love, we got home to find it all here and instantly started putting dinner together. Hadrian felt the need to hover while I prepped it for the oven."

"I wasn't hovering," he whined, but I rolled my eyes.

Leo's voice was so vulnerable and borderline childlike as he asked, "So you are okay with staying here?"

Stepping close to him, I tilted my head up to look at him as his hands rested on my hips. "We are staying."

"Good." He leaned forward and kissed me softly, then he swatted me on the ass, pulling an involuntary moan from me. No one had been able to do that other than these two men, the first of which stepped behind Leo and wrapped his hands around him, slipping his hand to rest on his stomach. The heat in Leo's eyes seared me in place. "Now, go unpack. Take over however much of the closet you want."

"Okay."

CHAPTER 6

LEO

Watching them take their luggage down the hall was surreal. My tom was pacing excitedly, and I had to mentally tell him to calm the fuck down while I stood there and marveled once again that this was not a hallucination. Inhaling, I took in Marie's sweet scent mixed with Hadrian's rich whiskey. I tried to hide the fear that they didn't want to stay here, but I couldn't help the tremble in my hands when I touched her. When they assured me they did want to be here, it took all my political training not to sag in relief. So instead, I brought forward the confident swagger. I took another deep breath, letting their scents wrap around me and remind me I had found my mates. Found the other pieces of my soul.

Three quick, rhythmic knocks sounded at the door and I groaned. What in the fucking hell did Masen want now? Couldn't he give me just one night?

When I turned and opened the door, Masen was leaning against the pole with his back to me. I groaned. This wasn't good. Matching him on the other support to the porch, I asked, "What did the scouts find?"

"It's the Los Padres Pride. King Ivan still wants Ronni back because apparently, Prince Kaiden now wants to claim her."

"Seriously? Ending Edwin the way we did wasn't enough?"

A dangerous growl came from Masen as he said, "Apparently, he believes the twins should be his, not mine."

"I'll get the guards to protect the house at all times. She'll be protected, Mase. No one is getting to the cubs."

"I know the pride will protect her. We have had some small outbursts in the last three years, but I don't want another war on our people."

"Marie and Hadrian will take care of Ronni if that happens. You know that the guard, Mom and Dad, and the rest of this pride will protect her."

Masen only moved his eyes toward me but asked, "She's in that bad of shape, isn't she?"

"Doc was right, Prince Masen. Princess Ronni will need to have a c-section for delivery, and likely before term. It's too risky for her and the cubs," Marie said from behind us. "Sorry, Leo. We were done, and I came out and overheard that Los Padres is threatening the cubs?"

Masen looked at me and then jerked his head toward the house. We went inside, and when we sat on the couch, she sat next to me and said, "I'm sorry for eavesdropping."

"It's okay, Marie."

"It's not. I didn't want to scare Princess Ronni earlier, but one of the many reasons for bed rest is because . . ." She looked at Masen, who looked completely terrified. "It's called placental abruption. It's rare, but the placenta, which feeds the cubs all they need, is separating from the uterine wall."

"If it completely separates, what happens to Ronni and the cubs?" Masen asked carefully.

Hadrian came to sit on the arm of the sofa next to me and their eyes met for a long moment before she turned to Masen. She studied him for a moment, and her face morphed from my mate looking at her brother-in-law to the doctor she was.

"You have to tell him."

"I know, Hadrian." She took a deep breath and met Masen's gaze. "For Ronni, clotting, extreme blood loss. For the cubs, possibility of a stillbirth due to lack of nutrients and oxygen."

Panic filled Masen's eyes. "I could lose them all?"

"Not if I have anything to say about it. She needs to stay on bed rest for as long as possible. We will need her to stay put with low stress for another few weeks. If we can give the cubs two more weeks to grow and develop, it will be better." She stood up and started pacing, in deep thought. "We just have to balance it with Princess Ronni's health. I'll be checking in every day. If she starts to feel nauseated, has any bleeding, or becomes too weak, get me immediately. I'll talk to Doc about getting a set of equipment moved into the house."

Her head popped up to look at Masen. "Sorry, I'm assuming you'd be okay with that."

"Anything you need to keep my family whole." He stood and pulled her into a tight hug. "Welcome to the family." Her focus went to me, and I saw the tears line her eyes. When he stepped away, his voice was low. "Thank you for everything."

"It's my job."

Masen shook his head. "I don't mean what you are doing for Ronni. I mean for Leo. Thank you."

She swallowed, and her focus went back to me as he walked out the door. Marie studied me, and when my eyebrows pinched together, she said, "I'm breaking all the confidentiality laws when it comes to telling you and Masen this."

"However, while we have our license with the state of California, we technically have to follow Ashstrike's laws, which allow us to provide information to mates," Hadrian explained.

"I don't want to scare them, but I really am worried about the princess. Typically, I would want to wait a month before planning the cesarian, getting her as close to full term as possible."

"It's that bad?" My heart rate sped up.

My attention went to Hadrian, who had moved to the cushion on the couch before he leaned forward on his knees and let out a long sigh. My tom was bristling. "Hadrian?"

I swallowed, looking between them. They studied each other, and I drew in a long breath before I said, "No secrets in this house between the three of us. If this is going to work, there can be no secrets."

Hadrian looked at me and his lips thinned. "Even under Ashstrike, there will be times when we won't be able to tell you everything because there are still laws protecting patient confidentiality. It's going to be the same thing when it comes to pride matters for you, love. We respect that, and we need you to respect that portion for us as well."

I tried to tap down on the pride laws of protecting my princess that were roaring beneath the surface. I could even feel my tom turning toward it and growling against its pressures. I stood and rolled my neck and shoulders, trying to let it go.

"Leo," Marie said quietly, and I held a finger up and said as easily as I could, "Hold on a moment and I will explain."

It took another few breaths before I could calm my racing heart and let my tom handle the fight with pride law. My skin tingled, and I concentrated on not letting my claws loose. It helped that they patiently allowed it and that both of them just watched me.

After another moment, I turned and leaned against the wall, looking at one of the pictures of Mase, Morgan, and me when we were about ten years old. "When Morgan and I came of age, we vowed our allegiance to the Ventana Wilderness Pride and to Crown Prince Masen Cartwell. That bound me by pride law, just as tightly as the bloodline ties Masen. In fact, when he realized Ronni was his mate, he couldn't tell her because of that bloodline. Morgan and I were not able to either."

I met Marie's gaze that had turned tender. "So, when I am protective of Ronni, it isn't just because I truly feel like she is my sister. I am law bound to protect her. My very cells will want to protect Masen and Ronni, just as they will want me to protect you." I felt the lump sit hard in my throat as a strong hand landed on my cheek, and I flicked my focus to Hadrian. Tears escaped my eyes, but I made myself say, "Please do whatever you can to not put me in a position that I would ever have to choose which direction to go? I finally found you. My *mates*. The other pieces of my soul."

Marie's hand took mine, and they both whispered, "Okay."

I kissed Hadrian and Marie quickly and took another deep breath. "Now, can you please tell me just how bad Princess Ronni is so my tom will stop growling?"

Marie pulled me back to the couch. "Like I said, in a perfect world, those babes would stay right where they are until they are full term. Only the problem is where the placenta is located. Doc and I went over the reports this morning. It's attached to one of the worst areas of scarring in her uterus and is slowly detaching. I will need to do an ultrasound every couple of days to monitor it. From what they said, I'm hoping that we will make it another two weeks, but neither Doc nor I are sure it will be viable that long."

My chest caved in as the air left my lungs. I tried to force myself to breathe, but I just stared at her. She was trying to be the professional giving bad news, but I saw the heartbreak there in her eyes. My tom was whimpering, and I felt the band of pride law around my chest clutching tight. It pressed against my very essence to protect her, to keep her alive and well. After a couple of attempts, I finally was able to take a shuddering breath and let it out slowly. "Will she die?"

Her chin raised, and her voice was strong and determined. "If I have anything to say about it, she *and* both babes will live. Their heartbeats are strong, and Princess Ronni certainly appears to have a fight in her." A smile crossed her face as she said, "It helps that her new sister- and brother-in-law are the best in the state for delivering shifter babes. We travel all over to help with high-risk pregnancies. The only one we couldn't save was a bear mom who had been mauled by the babe's father. She was gone when we arrived, but we saved the cub, and it was placed with a very loving family."

That seemed to settle me a bit. I looked at Hadrian, and he said, "I promise, love. We will do everything we possibly can to ensure that the three of them live long, healthy lives."

"Thank you." The timer went off in the kitchen, and Hadrian went to pull dinner out of the oven. Marie came to sit down next to me, and I wrapped an arm around her. "And thank you for making dinner."

"Of course." She kissed my cheek and leaned her head on my shoulder. When she let out a long breath, I wrapped an arm around her shoulders, rubbing my thumb back and forth as she curled up into me. Her hair smelled like hot brown sugar as I rested my head on hers and took another calming breath. It only enhanced her scent, and I felt my soul calm, like a tight knot had unraveled from deep in my chest. We sat there like that for a long while before Hadrian stuck his head around the corner.

"Baby. Love. The table is set."

Marie got up, but I sat there a moment longer, needing to gather my thoughts. Hadrian kissed Marie's forehead, and I heard them talking in the other room but was too consumed in my own head to pay too close attention. We should be allowed to have private conversations, without concern for anyone else in the house.

I found not only my mate, but mates today. I trusted them enough to tell them just how tightly pride law bound me, so I would have to trust them to save my sister.

Rubbing my face, I took a deep breath at the overwhelming certainty that filled me: they already had that trust. They were professionals. If I couldn't trust them and they were the best in the state, then who could I? My tom growled at me.

I know. I know. But I only met them today.

Mates. He pushed back. *Trust in our mates.*

Just like that, I did. I felt my shoulders loosen at the thought. Warmth flowed through me, another sense of completeness loosening my breath.

When I faced the kitchen, they turned and smiled at me, and I saw nothing but warmth in their eyes. My heart expanded, and I knew that if this kept up, it wouldn't be long before I fell deeply in love with both of them.

Chapter 7
Hadrian

Letting Marie and Leo have a moment, I stood and went to get dinner out of the oven. After taking it out and setting it to cool on the stove, I leaned my palms flat on the counter to steady myself and breathe. Leo had a right to know how bad the princess was, but to see him struggle like that . . . *that* was hard. I wanted to just reach out and hold him, but I could tell there was something more. Something that we weren't seeing.

I wasn't sure at first if he was mad that we weren't telling him everything and that was why he was reacting the way he was, but watching him pull himself together was impressive. I had heard rumors that the hands to a royal family could be bound by special laws, but to hear him tell us about it . . . had my mind reeling. My mate was a force.

Then, Marie told him how we had come here *because* of her high-risk pregnancy. Sure, Doc was very sick and they shouldn't be near her, but there were other staff here that could have covered. No, Princess Ronni and the babes were why we were sent here. I took a deep breath and went to set the small table. After putting out the shredded lettuce, tomatoes, olives, and sour cream, I plated us each a section of Marie's famous taco lasagna. It was just taco meat, cheese, salsa, and tortillas, but there was something heavenly about it. It won everyone over every time.

Peeking through the doorway to the living room, I saw Marie leaning on Leo's shoulder and I smiled. I'd seen that woman have to deliver some really fucked-up news, and I couldn't imagine how she was feeling right now, knowing it was our mate that had been at the receiving end.

"Baby. Love. Table is set," I said quietly.

She got up and headed into the kitchen, pulled me just out of his view, took a deep shuddering breath, and leaned her forehead on my chest for a moment. "We've had to tell people we will do our best before, but that was so much harder. He's our mate, Hadrian. The thought of letting him down shreds me."

"I know, baby. We just have to do what we do best. Like you said, we will do an ultrasound every other day and monitor everything *very* closely. If it makes you more at peace, tell her not to be alone at any time. Even if she just has to go to the bathroom." Marie was right, though. The thought of letting Leo down hurt deeper than anything else I'd felt in my life. I kissed the top of her head, and she squeezed me tight and took a step back. "Let's get some food."

"He's struggling with having mates." She looked off toward where Leo sat on the couch, deep in thought.

"I think we surprised him. Not only did he find one mate, he found two. Both of us." Looking at where Leo was, I saw him tilt his head back and let out a long breath. "We never know when we'll find our mate, but it was probably extra jarring it happened in the middle of making sure our princess, his sister, successfully makes it through a pregnancy that could potentially kill her. It's our job to make sure we all live through this. After seeing the pain on his face as he worked through what we were saying, I'm not sure he would survive losing her. If he does, he won't be the same person."

When I looked back at Marie, she smiled at me. "Your ability to read people is amazing. I'm forever in awe of it."

We headed over to the table, and when we turned to look at Leo, he was looking at us with the sweetest smile on his face. I jerked my head for him to come to dinner, noting the heavy breath he let out and how his shoulders relaxed as he joined us.

When Leo finished making his additions to his dinner, he took a bite, and the moan from him was almost sinful. Smiling, Marie said, "No one can resist taco lasagna. It may not end wars, but it will get them to the table to talk their shit out."

"This is really good."

Getting cocky the way only she could, she shrugged. "I know. Now eat. You need your strength."

He raised his eyebrows as he took another bite. When he finished, he met her gaze and just said, "Do I now? Because I believe it's going to be *you* who needs it tonight."

I smirked and reached over to squeeze his leg. His hand lay on mine, and he said, "She's not the only one."

Heat flushed my face as I continued to eat. I tried to keep my mind from playing out what might happen later because I could see that Marie was shifting in her seat, and the scent of all our arousal was thick in the air.

Once Leo had finished his dinner, he sat there for a moment before starting to put the food away. His voice had dropped an octave before commanding, "You two, stay right there."

My eyes met Marie's, and she swallowed before just muttering, "Yes, sir." Her heat filled the room, and she squirmed in her seat again.

Leo smirked, and his shoulders lowered just slightly. We watched as he put away the leftovers and washed the pan. Once finished, he turned and leaned against the counter, ankles and arms crossed. Fuck, he was sexy as hell. His gaze ran over each inch of me, and when he didn't say anything, I bit my lip.

His focus went to Marie, where he looked her over with just as much intensity, and he licked his lips. "On your knees on the bed. Fully undressed." As she stood, he curled his finger, commanding her to him. "Come here first."

Her breathing hitched, and I couldn't help but smirk. She was loving every minute of this, and it made my cock hard and my tom whimper in anticipation. Leo reached out, wrapping his hand softly around her throat, and pulled her to him. The purred, "Mine," had me shifting in my seat. Then, he kissed her, and she grabbed onto his shirt, moaning into his mouth. The sound had me biting back a whimper.

There was nothing I enjoyed more than seeing her getting pleasured, whether by me or someone else. I couldn't wait to see her getting it from our mate. Fuck, I was a dead man.

She pulled back, and he jerked his head toward the bedroom. Turning, she looked at me flush-faced and wide-eyed as she hurried out. I watched her leave and then slowly looked to Leo, who was already staring at me.

Swallowing, I held his gaze.

"You . . ." He studied me. "What do *you* want?"

I blinked in surprise, and when I didn't answer, he came to stand before me, and I reached out, wrapping my hands around his calves. My eyes flicked to his cock pressing against his pants, but his hand wrapped around my throat and forced me to face him.

"Answer me, Hadrian."

My mouth watered at the single thought that went through my head. "I want you . . ."

"How?" He gently squeezed his fingers tighter and a flash of heat went through my entire body. Fuck, I'd always been the dominate one with Marie, and whenever we went outside our relationship, I'd still somehow always been the one giving the orders.

Leo grabbed my chin, his thumb rubbing along my bottom lip as my tongue snaked out and licked it. "I want you down my throat."

"Good boy."

I whimpered, straight whimpered, as my tom mimicked the sound. He pulled me up, kissed me softly, and then hummed. "You taste like rich whiskey. Can't wait to see if *all* of you tastes the same." He gave me another, harder kiss. "Now, move. We don't want to keep our queen on her knees, waiting."

CHAPTER 8

LEO

Watching Hadrian melt under me while we'd been in the kitchen was glorious. No man had ever made me or my tom feel so at ease. When we stepped into the bedroom, the most glorious sight lay before me.

Marie was on her knees, back to the headboard, her hands holding it behind her. The position had her chest pushed out, and the blush that rose in her cheeks trailed down her chest as well.

"Fuck," I drawled, and my mouth watered as my eyes trailed down her body and I saw her in her full magnificence.

Hadrian was quickly stripping next to me, and I reached back, pulled my T-shirt over my head, and undid my belt. By the time I was undressed, Hadrian was at the foot of the bed, on his knees. Without hesitation, they were both submitting to me. I knew there would need to be a discussion, but it was beautiful as fucking hell to see them like that.

My heart beat faster at the realization that my mates were here and waiting for me.

My mates.

I took the few steps to Hadrian, gripping the base of my cock and stroking it. The heat in his gaze and the way he licked his lips made me harder.

"I'm going to lie on this bed, and you are going to swallow me just like you said you wanted. Understand?" He nodded, and I leaned forward and kissed him hard. Swallowing his moan, I reached down and pumped him. It was sexy as fucking hell.

Lying on my back on the bed, I positioned myself between Marie's legs, ran a finger through her, inhaling her heat, and said, "You, baby, are going to sit down and ride my face until you can't hold yourself up anymore. Is that understood?"

Her breathy, "Yes, sir," was intoxicating. Reaching up and wrapping my arms around her waist, I pulled her down and licked from her ass to clit, flicking it. Her sweetness exploded on my tongue as she whimpered, "Oh my gods."

She tried to rise, and I growled. "I told you to sit, not hover. Now sit down and take your pleasure, baby."

When she complied, I moaned at the feel of her softness against my tongue as I teased the nerves around her entrance and back up to her clit.

When my tongue swept into her, Hadrian's ran along the length of my cock and I moaned. And when his lips wrapped around the head of me, slowly taking more and more into his mouth, I tried not to lose myself to it too quickly.

Marie's hips moved and rolled against me as she rode out her pleasure, and I couldn't keep my hips from thrusting up into Hadrian's mouth. I felt him adjust his position and then I slid down his throat. With short, quick thrusts, he took every inch of me.

Fuck. No one had taken me like this before. No one had given me the pleasure that rippled through me like this. This was something wholly different. Something all-consuming.

My tongue flicked and clamped onto Marie's clit, and her moan filled the room as she leaned forward, resting her hands on my chest. "Fuck, Leo. You should see how fucking amazing Hadrian looks, sucking your cock."

I pulled her clit farther into my mouth and flicked it with my tongue. Marie's groans filled the air, and Hadrian's chuckle vibrated around my cock as he pulled back. I thrust back into his throat, setting an even pace for him as he licked and sucked me with perfection.

I brought my hands around to Marie's ass, spread her cheeks wide, and licked my way down to her puckered hole but stopped short. When she whimpered, I pressed a finger against it as I dove into her entrance, feeling her already getting close.

"Fuck, Leo. Yes." She bounced, and I pressed my finger knuckle deep into her ass, her pussy instantly quivering at the pleasure ripping through her.

"That's right, baby. Come for me." My tongue swiped up and around her clit before diving back into her core, teasing all her pleasure points.

Her hands moved to rest on my ribs, and Hadrian lifted off my cock to swirl his tongue around. "Come on, baby. Give Leo what he wants. Coat his face in your sweetness."

Hearing him, I thrust my hips up, and he licked down my shaft to my balls, sucking them into his mouth. When I moaned, the vibrations sent her over the edge. Her screams of pleasure filled the room as she quivered and released all over my face. With a twitch of my finger, another wave hit her, my name a guttural sound as she screamed her pleasure. I licked up every inch of her to clean her up. After she collapsed next to me, I lifted my head to see Hadrian swallow me once again.

"Damn, you are right, baby. Hadrian looks sexy as fuck with my cock in his mouth."

"I'm a little jealous, love."

"You'll get your taste, but first Hadrian is going to swallow every drop."

His moan rolled through me, and I reached down, threading my hands through his hair and gripping him tight. I felt my release climbing, and when he deep-throated me again and slid a finger to my ass, my legs instinctually widened for him. My hips moved without conscious thought as I watched him blow me.

Marie came over and kissed me. My hand tightened in Hadrian's hair, and he moaned. "Fuck yes," was my only response before I released down his throat.

Hadrian swallowed every drop. When he finished cleaning me up, he stood, stroking his cock as Marie reached over and played with his balls. It was then I noticed the pubic piercing. I didn't get to admire it long before he grunted and my focus went back to his eyes. With his eyes holding mine, he moaned, "Mine," as he came hard, his seed spilling onto my stomach.

After he leaned on the bed, trying to hold himself up, I sat up and held his gaze as I bent down and licked him clean. His cock twitched and an indecent moan came from him when my lips wrapped around him.

When I released him with a pop, I came up, flicked a nipple with my tongue, and kissed him softly on the lips. Marie lay down, and I sucked in one of her nipples, flicking it with my tongue as well before I kissed her, muttering, "Be right back."

After cleaning everyone up, we crawled into bed, and I chuckled when they insisted I sleep between them. As I lay between my mates, they each turned and wrapped an arm around my stomach, resting their heads on my shoulders.

I kissed them each on the top of the head and savored the feel of them against me. My tom was on his back, sated and content once again. When Marie let out a long breath, kissing my shoulder, and Hadrian kissed the mating spot, I knew I was already falling hard and fast for these two.

CHAPTER 9
MARIE

Waking this morning between Leo and Hadrian was beyond anything I could have imagined. At some point in the night, Leo had wrapped an arm around me and sandwiched me tight between him and Hadrian, mumbling something about how he needed to have his hands on both of us.

My mind went back to last night as I lay there this morning. It was different being in bed with two mates. One might think that even though Hadrian and I had shared our bed, it would have been much the same having Leo there. They would be so wrong.

The orgasms were so much more intense, the feel of his tongue on mine setting my very skin alight. My queen mewled like a kitten with them. She'd been quiet as a church mouse with anyone else in our bed.

Looking at the two of them, I seriously debated crawling under the blankets and waking them up with their dicks in my mouth. Would Leo be okay with that? Hell, the way he just ordered me around last night had me ready to go instantly. I was just about to follow through on my thoughts when there was a knock on the door.

Leo was up with a pair of sleep pants on quicker than I could blink. The guard's voice was low, but not low enough that I couldn't hear.

"Prince Masen and Morgan are on the way as well."

Leo whispered, it wasn't like he was trying to keep it from us. "The king and queen don't want me to meet them at the house?"

"No, sir."

A moment later, the door shut, and Leo was standing in the doorway to the bedroom, rubbing his face. Was it possible for him to be better looking in the morning?

"Love?" I asked, sitting up. "What's going on?"

He headed for the bathroom and said, "I don't know. Apparently, Mom and Dad are coming over with Mase and Morgan."

Confused, I looked down to Hadrian, who also had a very puzzled look on his face. "Mom and Dad?"

He ran some water over his toothbrush and turned toward us, sighing. "I guess I didn't explain that part, did I?" He brushed his teeth quickly and then splashed some water on his face. After patting it dry, he leaned on the doorframe and Hadrian sat up in the bed.

"We are trying to be patient."

Leo shook his head. "In public, the king and queen are exactly that. The king and queen of the pride. However, whenever we are at their home, or at Masen's, Morgan's, or here, they are Mom and Dad. They don't allow us to call them anything but that. If we get formal in any way, even at our age, they will lay into us like we are two-year-old cubs."

"You mentioned yesterday that they had taken you in after your parents died." I was trying to put the puzzle together but still didn't really understand the whole picture. "But why are they coming here first thing in the morning?"

A sweet smile graced his face as he came to the edge of the bed and cupped my cheek in his hand. "To meet their new son and daughter, I'm sure. You are my mates, and I would be very surprised if they didn't personally welcome you to the family."

"So, no pressure for them to like us or anything," Hadrian said, climbing out of the bed and kissing my cheek.

I huffed a laugh and shook my head. "The guard said that they were on their way?" I asked, just as a knock sounded at the door.

Leo looked that way, his nose twitched, and he smiled and yelled out, "Since when do you and Masen knock?"

The door opened, and Leo turned back to me and said, "You two, get dressed, and I'll entertain these assholes."

"We can hear you, and if you need to get cleaned up, please do so," Masen hollered back, but then Morgan said, "Don't tempt Leo with that. He'll be an hour in the shower with those two."

I smiled because as I looked at the two of them on the bed, I could absolutely see myself worshiping both of them for the next hour. Leo tipped his head in agreement, and I felt the heat in my cheeks as a smirk cross Hadrian's face.

Leo grabbed a T-shirt and slipped it on as he headed out of the bedroom. He stopped short of the threshold, though, and strode back, kissing me. "Good morning, baby." Then, he turned to Hadrian and kissed him. "Good morning, handsome. Get cleaned up. I'll see you two out there soon."

I just smiled at him as he walked out, shutting the door behind him. There was a slightly muffled, "You two are the worst fucking brothers ever. Can't I sleep in with them for one fucking day before you come barging into the house?"

Hadrian laughed and asked, "We have inherited one hell of a family, haven't we?"

"We have." I let out a long breath, though, as the list of things that we now needed to do grew.

"Wonder if Katerina would be willing to box up our stuff and send it down here or if we will need to make a trip. I'm not really wild about leaving Leo, and him taking time off to help us move may not be in the cards."

"If Katerina can't, maybe Derrik can. I can head up by myself too, if you want to stay here with him."

"Don't you want to stay?"

He smiled as he looked at the bedroom door that led to the hallway. "Of course. I never want to leave him now that we've found him. I want to complete the mating, get settled, and work on integrating our lives together. We need to talk to Doc, too, and see if there is room for us at the clinic. We also need to talk to the king and queen and find out if it's going to be a problem with us still helping patients across the state. Hell, even just have a day with Leo where we can figure out life plans."

I thought about that statement, and I felt something within me shift. Where I had been content with life being our jobs and Hadrian for the last few years, there was this part of me screaming now. "Hadrian?"

When his focus found mine, I lowered my voice to the softest whisper, so hopefully they wouldn't hear in the main room. "Are cubs up for discussion?"

He blinked and looked in the direction of Leo, where he was laughing with his brothers as they lovingly razed him about us. Hadrian swallowed and came to stand in front of me. "If you and Leo want cubs, let's have cubs."

"That isn't what I asked." I met his gaze. "When we talked about it when we were first mated, you had said that you would discuss it after we had been together longer. I understood that because you were still coming to fully understand who you were. I also told you at the time that I was content with our work."

"And now, not only am I comfortable in my own sexuality, but I have both pieces of my soul." He smiled, cupped my head in his hands, and kissed me softly on the lips. "Do *you* want cubs?"

Staring into those blue eyes of his, I nodded. "Yeah, I think I do."

"Okay, because if you don't want them, end of discussion. But yes, I am willing to discuss the three of us having cubs. Leo needs to be on board. If not, then we have a different conversation."

I nodded and took a deep breath. He was right. This needed to be something the three of us sat down and talked about. While I was appreciative that if I didn't want them, the discussion was over, I also understood that it would be the three of us raising kids. Not just me. Not just him. Not just Leo. The three of us would be parents to those cubs, no matter which one of them biologically fathered them.

Standing, I took Leo's hand and pulled him to me. His arms wrapped around me, and he kissed the top of my head. "Love you, baby."

"Love you too, Hadrian."

CHAPTER 10

LEO

"**M**om, Dad, this is Marie and Hadrian. My mates." I smiled at each of them and when they bowed, I shook my head and huffed.

"Now, now. None of that. Stand up and give me a hug," Mom said, rushing toward Marie and wrapping her arms around her tightly. She released her, kissed her cheek, and then embraced Hadrian. I couldn't help the even bigger smile that crossed my face. When Mom pulled back from him, though, she kissed his cheek and turned toward me, finger out and eyes narrowed. "Leo, didn't you tell them that in this family, we don't bow to each other?"

"I did, Mom, but they are showing respect."

"He did, ma'am." Hadrian's voice was strong but tentative.

Marie tilted her head to the side in a very feline manner as she asked, "Why wouldn't we bow to you?"

Dad smiled and stepped forward to stand in front of them. "Leo is as much our son as is Masen. He's bound by the same royal pride law, and so, as his mates, we ask you to behave as he does with us. When we are in our homes, we are simply Mom and Dad."

"That's what Leo said, but . . ."

He raised an eyebrow at her. "You didn't believe your mate?"

"It's not that, sir. It's just . . . I've never met a king and queen who differentiate," she said carefully, and I admired the fact that she questioned everything.

"We do things a little differently here, Dr. Fuller." He stood tall and became every ounce the king of the pride he was, but when Marie held his gaze, he cracked a smile.

"Dad . . . ," I whined, but Marie nodded, and I reached over and wrapped an arm around her, kissing her temple.

"If you are to be Mom and Dad, please call me Marie."

A wicked gleam shone in Dad's eye as he looked at me and smirked. "I was only showing you the respect of your position."

I shook my head at him, and Marie chuckled next to me. "Okay, that's fair, but my statement stands. I think I can speak for Hadrian as well."

"Oh, by the gods. Yes, please. Do *not* call me Nurse Fuller." His nose wrinkled, and it was so freaking adorable. "Hadrian is fine."

Dad's attention went to me, and I just smiled at the two of them, seeing nothing but pride on their faces. Mom's eyes met mine, and when I saw them lined with tears, I could tell she wanted to know if I was happy. Smiling at her, I nodded. "Yes, Ma."

I felt more than saw my mates look at me in question. Mom merely nodded. I knew she just wanted me to be happy, and in this moment, I was ecstatic.

"Well," Dad said, "welcome to the family." He put a hand to his chest and nodded to each of them.

Morgan sighed and flopped on the couch and huffed a laugh. Dad, however, smirked and shook his head at him. "I don't know why you are getting comfortable, Morgan."

"I'm sorry?"

A conspiratorial grin crossed his face as he looked at Masen and asked, "Angelica with Ronni?"

Morgan and Masen's eyes narrowed in unison as they said, "She is."

"Good, because I have some recon I need you two to do today."

My confused gaze went to him. Usually, I was the one doing recon. Their attention went to me, and Mom was the one who said, "You, Leo, will be spending the day with your mates. You can resume your usual duties tomorrow."

"But if there is recon to do, that is going to take Mase away from Ronni. Is that smart right now?"

Mom looked to Marie and Hadrian. "Based on your observations yesterday, is Ronni okay for her husband *and* you two to be away today?"

Marie looked to Hadrian and then the floor. I could see the conflict in her eyes. She was trying to figure out how much to tell them. With a deep breath, my mate stood tall again. "As long as we, and I mean Hadrian and I, aren't gone more than a few hours. The PA can handle most anything that could go wrong."

I squeezed her side, and Hadrian reached over and wrapped his arm around her as well. It was the best possible answer. "I think we can stay close and only be out of town for a few hours."

My gaze went to Masen, and he nodded. "Please, spend time with them."

"I usually do the recon, though."

I looked at Dad, and he just stared at me with nothing but love and respect in his eyes as he said, "They can handle this. You need to spend time with Marie and Hadrian. Please take one day off."

He held my gaze, and when he lifted an eyebrow, I knew he was calling me out on rarely taking a day for myself. Nodding, I ran through locations that I wanted to show them that would still be close enough should something happen and we need to get back. "We will head northwest. Garrapata. If anything happens, send a guard to the river at the break. We should be able to be back here in an hour."

Hadrian's hand moved to my hip, and his thumb moved back and forth, soothing me ever so slightly. "She should be fine today. She was stable yesterday."

"I'd . . ." Marie looked up at me. I saw the turmoil in her gaze. She was trying really hard to agree to this, and I nodded. "I'd like to check in on her before we go. I really want to spend the day with you, Leo, and get to know my mate and have you get to know us. But I have a duty to her."

"Okay, baby. Before we head out, we will go check on Ronni. If you see anything that concerns you, then we will stay closer to town so that we can be available if needed. There are a couple of smaller waterfalls that I want to eventually show you two as well, so whether that is today or in a week, it doesn't matter."

Relief shone in her eyes, and Hadrian nodded in agreement.

Ronni was feeling well, the babies were doing great, and there had been no changes since the day before.

So, after heading out of town, shifting, and weaving through the forest for about an hour, we made it to the area near Garrapata I wanted to show them. Marie was leaning forward and getting a drink of water as I prowled toward her. Hadrian's nose twitched, and I saw the mischief in his eyes as I launched into the air, latching onto her neck and rolling with her into the water. There was a yip in the air as Hadrian joined us. Marie came up gasping. After shifting, she splashed us both and said, "You jerks!"

I huffed a laugh before Hadrian and I both shifted and swam over to the river's edge. Marie leaned back, lying flat on the shore, and I crawled up her body, kissing her stomach, her collarbone, up her neck before lifting my head and smiling at her.

Her eyes narrowed, and then she put a hand on my cheek and purred, "You're lucky you are cute."

"He's lucky you are his mate. She would have clawed your face off if you were anyone else, cute or not." He sat down next to us as I held myself over Marie's body.

Leaning down, I kissed her quickly before sitting back and looking at them. My fingers trailed in the dirt, and my mind started spinning with what I wanted to know about them. My eyes lifted to look at them, and they cocked their heads to the side. Marie sat up, leaning on her hands just behind her as she asked, "What do you want to know?"

"How did you meet?"

Hadrian smiled. "I was hanging at a bar in Reno, saw her dancing, and here we are."

Marie laughed. "Seriously, you aren't going to tell him how you had a full identity crisis? How it took me six months of proving to you that I didn't give a shit about who you wanted in your bed, as long as it was me with you as well? That I was flexible and earned your trust? That I had to do all that before you would mate me?"

His cheeks reddened. "For the record, it wasn't that I didn't trust you. I did. It was me I didn't trust."

I smiled at him. "I understand that. When I realized I didn't care who I ended up with, whether they be male or female or neither, it was a bit unsettling. I worried that I wouldn't be accepted. Worried that I would be shunned by the pride. I was lucky, though, because Masen and Morgan supported me. Mom and Dad held me as I cried when I told them. They just said they loved me and just wanted me happy. As word got out in the pride, there were a few problems, but my position squashed a lot of it."

"My parents didn't really care, but my grandparents disowned me." Hadrian shrugged nonchalantly, but there was sadness in his eyes. "It was easy to distance myself. I always thought I would work for my parents' construction company, but after I finished high school, I realized there weren't enough medically trained people to help others in my area. So, I went and got my nursing degree, met Marie, and the rest is history."

When I reached over and rested my hand on Marie's leg, her attention was fixed on Hadrian. The love in her eyes for him warmed my soul. "Why did you become a doctor, baby?"

Her eyes dimmed slightly, and I saw the sadness in Hadrian's face before she said, "Like many who go into the medical field, I had a family member die. I was sixteen when my mom was diagnosed with interstitial lung disease." I furrowed my brows, and she sighed. "Basically, her lungs scarred over until she wasn't able to breathe. It was hard to watch, and I wanted to help others. After I passed the boards, I found I really enjoyed bringing life into the world. Found out I was really good at it, too. Since then, we've specialized and celebrated lots of shifters births."

"I'm sorry you had to witness your mom die. What about your dad?"

She took a deep breath and let it out slowly. "He couldn't live without my mom. Their bond was so deep, he died of a broken heart just a few months later. Went to bed one night and didn't wake up."

Marie stared at her feet for a few minutes, and we just sat there in silence. It wasn't uncomfortable. We lounged on the bank, listening to the sounds of the forest around us and soaking up the rays of sun that shone through the tree branches overhead. I had tilted my head back, eyes closed, just breathing in the scent of my mates and sounds of the forest. It was peaceful. Marie's voice broke through the silence. "Leo?"

When I lifted my head to look at her with a raised eyebrow in question, she didn't say anything at first but gnawed on her bottom lip. "What is it, baby?"

"What are your thoughts on cubs?"

Cubs? Damn. My attention went to Hadrian for a moment, and he lifted his eyebrows in question as well. They had discussed it but obviously wanted my input. "That is really a question for you. Do you want cubs?"

Hadrian started giggling. "Told you."

"What?"

"I gave her almost the exact same answer when she asked me this morning."

I gave them both a confused look. "You haven't talked about cubs before?"

Marie blushed and Hadrian was beaming at our queen. "Well, we did, but at the time, neither of us were in mental states to bring a cub into the world. When she brought it up again this morning, I told her it was really up to her."

Nodding, I looked at her. "So, do you want cubs?"

The red in her cheeks brightened as she met my gaze. "Yeah, I think I might be ready for cubs, but only if both of you are on board with it. Regardless of who provides the DNA, you will both be their fathers."

"Naturally," Hadrian said, smiling at me.

She met my gaze and asked again, "Do *you* want cubs?"

A large smile crossed my face as I looked at my mates and saw their eyes alight with the possibility of expanding our family. "I hadn't found my mates, so I didn't think cubs were a possibility for me. I was content being Uncle Leo forever. Now that I've found you, yes, I think I would love to have cubs."

She nodded, tears lining her eyes. Getting up, I leaned over her and kissed her. "My only request is for us to take it one day at a time. Let's get *us* settled first. I don't want to rush the mating. I need you two to be sure of me, know me for me. I can't wait to mate you, and when we are ready, we can talk some more about timing."

CHAPTER 11

MARIE

TWO DAYS LATER

The last two days had been a roller coaster. Four others had also come down with pneumonia, and we were quarantining them in their homes. This string was roaring through the pride, and I was having to place another order for antibiotics. Doc was starting to feel better and wasn't contagious anymore, but he was still working on getting his energy back and had a lingering cough.

Not to mention the fact that word had spread that Hadrian and I were Leo's mates. We had been welcomed with open arms, but it also made people more likely to come into the clinic. Minor things people wouldn't normally come in for were rampant, like allergies, cuts that had almost healed by the time I saw them, and I thought the most ridiculous one was the guy who came in for a splinter. They just had to meet the Doc and her nurse. Our staff was trying to filter through most of them as they were brought in, but the most persistent were seated in a room.

Sitting here in my office, I was finishing up paperwork while Hadrian cleaned up and discharged a couple of patients. When we were done, we were going to stop by Prince Masen and Princess Ronni's to check on her.

My door opened, closed, and I thought I heard the lock engage just as the sweet smell of Leo wrapped around me. I didn't look up, but it wasn't long before he was leaning over the back of my chair and nuzzling his nose into my neck, kissing me there, and I hummed. "Hey, baby."

"Leo."

His arms wrapped around me and settled on my stomach. They moved slowly, lazily. "How much time do you need to finish up?"

"On my last one. Going to have to wait for Hadrian before we head over to Masen and Ronni's."

He spun my chair around and leaned down to look me in the eye. "Saw Hadrian already. Said he was going to be at least twenty to thirty minutes. Suggested I should come in here and . . ." He looked down the length of my body, heating me in all the right places. I shifted, feeling myself craving him already. "Keep you entertained."

"Really? And do you have any ideas on how to entertain me?"

His hand slowly drifted up my leg, his fingers sending goose bumps in their wake, before turning the chair so I was facing the computer. "I have a few ideas. First, you need to finish your work." His hand slid across my hip, over my center, and pushed against me. I couldn't help the squeak that came out.

As I was blinking and trying to focus on Mr. Balko's information, his hand slid into my pants and down to cup me completely, obliterating any focus I had. "Leo." I wanted his name to come out as a warning, but even I heard the heat in my voice, the plea for him to take me over.

His hand sat there, his middle finger occasionally running through me and pressing on my clit. Slow, careful movements that had my head swimming were making it ridiculously hard to concentrate. It took me twice as long to get all my notes in the system.

Once I hit submit on the chart, Leo removed his hand, whirled the chair around, and put my head in his hands as he kissed me. His tongue danced with mine, and I couldn't help but reach up and bunch up his tee in my fingers. He pulled back and whispered against my lips, "Do you have any idea how stunning you are?"

Feeling a little cheeky, I smirked. "Hadrian may have mentioned it a few times."

Leo's growl went right to me, and I swore I felt it vibrate my clit. There may have been a small whimper that left my lips, but he just said, "Not going to lie that I'm a little jealous that you've had time together. Guess I just need to make up for what I've missed."

His lips moved to kiss down my neck as one of his hands wrapped around my jaw. My words were breathless as he licked around Hadrian's mating mark, and I couldn't help that I bowed my back toward him in need. "We have each other now."

He hummed an agreement, pressed his lips to that mark again, and the next thing I knew, I was sitting on my desk with Leo pulling my pants down my legs, kissing along my thighs and calves in the process. Throwing my shoes, pants, and panties to the side, he grabbed both of my legs, spread me wide, and ran a wide tongue over me as he dove in.

"You taste fucking delicious, baby." He flicked my clit, and I couldn't stop my hips from moving against him, the scruff of his beard enticing every nerve to come alive. He slid two fingers into me and sucked on my clit, rolling it around his tongue.

My breathing and moaning were out of control. When I looked down at him, his eyes met mine as he lifted his head and commanded, "Coat my face so that I'll be tasting you all night, baby."

His fingers curled against my G-spot, and he licked and sucked every inch of me. My hand threaded through his hair as he continued his ministrations. God, the man knew how to use his tongue. When he explored within me, I gasped at just how deep he was as his thumb flicked and teased my clit.

"Leo." I moaned into the space as he lifted his head, sweeping his tongue along me again.

"Yes, baby? What do you need?" He kissed my inner thigh, trailing his tongue in circles before he mimicked it on the other one. My hips moved toward him involuntarily. A breathy chuckle came from him as he sucked me in again, rolling his tongue over me, against the pallet of his mouth, and slid three fingers into me.

"Fucking hell, love." Feeling myself skirting the edge of that pinnacle, I groaned as he curled his fingers against that spot one more time. With another swipe of his fingers, I fell into bliss, calling out Leo's name.

As I came down, trying bring myself back to reality, he licked me clean and slipped his fingers up to his mouth. The sight of it had me sucking in my bottom lip. It was incredibly hot. I was undoing his belt, not taking my eyes off him. Slowly, holding his gaze, I unbuttoned his jeans and then slowly lowered the zipper. His growl reverberated through the room, and I smirked.

"Baby likes to tease."

A light chuckle bubbled out of me as he nipped my lower lip, and I slid his jeans down over his hips. When I wrapped my hand around his cock and pumped, his head tipped back. When I slipped off the edge of my desk and went to drop to my knees, he caught me by the arms and lifted me, so I had to wrap my legs around him.

"I'm not going to last long. Watching you come undone . . . put me on edge, and I want to have my cum leaking out of you tonight." Pushing me against the wall, he wrapped his arms around my thighs, slid through my pussy a few times before he lined himself up to my entrance. My damn queen was caterwauling and begging for him.

"Look at me, baby."

I had work to keep my eyes from rolling into the back of my head at the feel of him against me. Looking into his blue eyes, though, I knew I was home. There was love and acceptance, and I felt cherished in his grasp, all while on the edge of sanity. There was so much intensity to it, I felt a knot build in my throat. Holding my gaze, he slowly slid into me. As I bit my lip, my nails dug into his shoulder as he filled me completely. With the restraint of a god, he dragged out of me and pushed back in. It was agonizing, yet such a turn-on. His focus hadn't left mine.

"Fuck, you feel amazing around me. I'm never going to get enough of you." His voice was a whispered prayer, and it made my nipples harden.

"Never enough," I whispered as he slowly picked up the pace, teasing every nerve along me, curving his hips to hit my overly sensitive G-spot. How lucky could I be to have two mates who could satisfy me so wholly?

With each continued thrust, he slammed in harder. I felt the coiling deep in my stomach, and my clit sparked with each connection of us.

He leaned forward and licked along the mating mark, and I spasmed around him. His groan and the swelling of his cock as he got closer told me all I needed to know. "Fuck me, Leo."

He did just that, and when he licked the mating mark again, I flew over the edge. Two more strokes and Leo was joining me in that bliss.

The world slowly formed back around us, and I lifted my head to look at my mate, smiling. "Well, I can say I was entertained."

The doorknob jiggled, and then there was a key turning the lock.

CHAPTER 12

HADRIAN

Just about everyone was out of the clinic when Leo came in, gave me a quick kiss, and I sent him in with Marie. We had all been so tired over the last few days that we would go to bed and just pass out. We would wake up in each other's arms, but we were so exhausted, we hadn't really had a chance to have much in the way of sex since we arrived, let alone talk about actually mating. Gods, I couldn't wait to mate Leo. Sure, we had that glorious first night, where I vividly recalled the taste of Leo on my lips, and a few hot moments here and there, but I wanted him to experience Marie coming undone under him. I wanted to experience coming undone under him.

I could hear Leo in her office doing exactly that. I had really hoped he had caught my meaning when I asked him to go entertain her. She had been really stressed and needed a release, and I was too busy trying to finish cleaning and preparing the rooms for tomorrow to be able to help her out. Leo and I had looked at each other and groaned when we heard her masturbating in the shower this morning. We had all overslept, and so we were to divide and conquer on the morning duties.

I couldn't wait to spend more time with him in the bedroom. Pulling the paper down to cover the bed, I wondered if he would order me to my knees or bend me over and take me. Fuck, I would do either for that man. When we asked if he would always want to be in control in the bedroom, he said he had always taken and enjoyed that role. Marie had explained she loved giving power over to someone else at the end of the day. She was the one in charge at work and having to make the tough calls, so she was more than willing to give both of us her full submission in whatever facet we wanted.

Leo had looked at me, and I shrugged. "I've always ended up the dominant one. But when you commanded me to my knees . . ." I bit my lip and hardened for him instantly. "It was as natural as breathing. I will give *you*, and only you, my submission, Leo."

I shook my head and pushed the thoughts away to finish up my work. It was only another five minutes before I heard them moan in ecstasy. After signing a few more things off, I slowly walked down the hall to her office and pulled out my keys to unlock it.

When I opened the door, the scent of their arousal hit me hard in the face and my dick came to full attention. I couldn't help but smile when I saw Leo's bare ass with Marie's legs wrapped around his hips. I had to take a hard breath and will my cock to keep from exploding from the sight. Though . . . I could still have fun.

"Hadrian, you couldn't give us just another minute?" Marie teased.

"I heard my mates' orgasm." I wiggled my eyebrows and twitched my nose, taking in more of the scent of them. "Can smell it, too."

Walking over, I gave them each a quick kiss and then bent down to get Marie's pants and panties. Leo slowly let her down, and I bit back a moan from watching him slide from inside her. When Leo reached for a tissue, I took his hand and shook my head.

As I went to my knees between them, my tom was purring loud enough, I thought I felt my chest rumble as I threw Marie's leg over my shoulder and licked her clean. The taste of both her and Leo's release was an explosion on my tongue, and I groaned against her as I lapped it all up.

"Fucking hell." She moaned as Leo chuckled and gave her a kiss.

"Hey, I wanted her to be leaking my cum tonight." He let out a heavy sigh and smiled at Marie. "Guess Hadrian felt a little left out."

Once she was adequately clean, I turned and licked away the remnants on Leo, sucking his softening cock into my mouth, making him groan.

As I stood, I ran my tongue over my lips and smiled at them. "Yeah, but who has both of their mates' tastes on their tongue?"

The wink I gave Leo had him shaking his head and smiling as he handed Marie her pants. "Let's go check on Mase and Ronni."

Ten minutes later, we were at their house, Masen welcoming us with warm hugs and Ronni trying very hard not to get up and get us something to drink. With just a narrowed eye from Masen, she leaned back into the couch. It was still weird not to use their titles, but they had insisted since we were family.

We followed her into the spare room, where we had all the equipment set up, and checked her over. After examining the placenta, Marie and I shared a look. It was continuing to dislodge along the worst of the scarring.

"Any bleeding?" Marie asked as she kept her eyes on the screen, moving the handpiece around to look at the cubs, who appeared to be doing well.

Ronni shook her head. "No. I'm tired, but I haven't seen any bleeding or spotting."

I looked at Masen, and he nodded his head in agreement. While I didn't need to know just how much they were doing in the bedroom, I figured he would be able to notice anything if they were.

I made a few notes as Marie dictated a few key points and then started cleaning Ronni up. As she pulled her dress back down over her belly and the twins, Marie sighed. "I don't think you are going to make it full term. I'd like to schedule your cesarean for next week. From what I'm seeing here, you should be fine until then. Anything longer and I think it's a roll of the dice. And when it comes to babies and mommas, I don't like to gamble."

Masen's throat bobbed, and I saw Leo stiffen out of the corner of my eye by Ronni's head. Ronni was looking only at Marie for a long minute and asked, "What do those dice look like?"

Marie held her gaze. "There's no issue at all going another week. You could be fine going longer . . . or you could start hemorrhaging. It becomes a lot more risky."

Ronni ran her hand over where the twins were waiting and growing. I flicked my gaze to Leo, whose shoulders were tight, and worry lined his eyes. I wanted so badly to wipe it away, have his eyes shine with the satisfaction that was in them back at Marie's office, only there was nothing I could do. Marie was right. It could go either way.

Ronni looked at Masen, and they just stared at each other, having a conversation in that way that people who truly loved each other could. Her voice broke the silence. "One week. Okay."

I saw the sag of relief in Marie's shoulders as they discussed the strategy and planning for it.

Thirty minutes later, the three of us were saying our goodbyes and heading home.

Stepping into the street, Marie reached over and threaded her fingers through both of ours. "I hate that part of my job."

"Telling someone they have to make a choice that could go perfectly or horribly wrong?" Leo asked.

She nodded, and I took a deep breath. "One week. Let's keep those babes where they are for a week. Even though they are shifters and are more resilient, they are still infants. Their lungs will be much better off if we can give them just one more week."

"It's a balance between the twins and Ronni, isn't it?" Leo asked carefully with his voice low.

"Yeah, it is. I promise you, Leo, we will do whatever we can to ensure you have a long life with all of them."

CHAPTER 13

LEO

I woke the next morning with my hand cupping Marie's pussy and Hadrian's hand around my cock, his hardness against me. When Marie moved and moaned, I knew we were all going to be late for work that day.

An hour later, and twenty minutes late to my meeting with the king and council, I strolled in to the king giving me a raised eyebrow, a twitch of his nose, and a shake of the head.

"Please tell me you have mated those two," he teased.

"Marie's beautiful, and Hadrian is a very handsome man. I'm surprised that after finding them all these years, you haven't mated them already," Council Member Griffon commented, leaning on her elbows on the table.

I shook my head. "I want them to know me. To bond with me willingly. It's not like when they mated. They had options on where to go and what to do. I'm a hand to the crown prince, bound by royal law. Want to make sure they fully think that through. I couldn't ask for better mates, and I do want to. I just want to make sure they want me for me, not just because the gods chose us to be together."

Vicar Hallsworth smiled. "The gods put us with people who match us. Who complete us. You *are* what they need, just as much as they are what *you* need."

Nodding, I swallowed and looked at Masen and Morgan sitting across from me. They smiled softly, and I took a deep breath. "I apologize for being late, Your Majesty. What is the topic of discussion today?"

"Los Padres." Morgan groaned.

"What is our next move? Masen said that they want the twins, but it will be a cold day in hell if that ever happens, that I will send them to with my own claws if I have to."

There was a murmur of agreement around the room, and Masen smiled in thanks. It was one of the other council members, though, that suggested cutting off their supplies.

Masen looked at his dad and shook his head. "I don't want to hurt the people of their pride. The king and prince? Sure. Burn them both for all I care, but they have been taught and led by King Ivan, who is vile on a good day."

"The people there treated Ronni like shit, Mase," I told him carefully.

He nodded. "I just don't want to give that order. We are better than that. King Ivan? Prince Kaiden? Yes. The people? No. I can't vote for that."

"How else are we supposed to stop this?" someone down the table demanded at the same time as another closer asked, "We are never going to get rid of the Los Padres Pride, are we?"

The king looked at them and said, "Not unless we take them over and eradicate them, including the king."

"Not only would that bring the agency down on us, but it would also not be what we stand for. We've never wanted to expand our land. There is no need to," Morgan tried to explain.

"Can they just let my mate go and let us live *our* lives?" Masen was starting to get twitchy, and I narrowed my eyes at him. He shook his head but rolled his neck. Morgan put a hand on his shoulder, and he relaxed.

I sighed and reminded him, "Remember, they believe we worked with the fae to destroy them."

"Well, that has recently been proven wrong with everything that happened with the fae. I mean, not sad that Angelica's father finally met his demise, but . . . I just want it to stop."

There were murmurs of agreement around the room.

CHAPTER 14

HADRIAN

Two days later, we had just finished dinner and were settling in for the night, but I felt antsy. It had been a pretty busy day, so I had taken a shower to wash the stress away, hoping I could reset and enjoy my evening with Marie and Leo.

I had just sat down on the couch when there was a knock on the door. Leo answered it to see that one of the councilman's guards asked if Marie would be willing to come and take a look at his cub, whose fever wouldn't break.

"Hadrian, you can stay here. Both of us don't need to go."

"You sure?" I was still reaching for my go bag, and she put her hand on my shoulder.

"Yes." She looked at Leo and I noted the glint in her eye. "Go for a run with Leo. I know how much you love to run under the stars."

Heat filled my cheeks as she kissed me and then, on her way out, kissed Leo and murmured something in his ear. His eyes flicked to me and held my focus as the heat rose in them.

"We will be back in a couple of hours. Be a good girl, baby," he told her with a swat to her ass and she headed out the door. Turning to me, he said, "Let's go. Baby gave us orders. We should follow them."

"I thought you were the one in charge?" I smirked as he also swatted my ass and pushed me toward the door. "You know I am. Now go outside and shift."

Taking a shuddering breath, I did as he said, and once my feet hit the soft dirt, my vision became clear in the darkness. I had to wait only a few seconds before the scent of Leo drew near. He leaned close and whispered in my ear, scratching under my jaw, "Good boy."

I purred and swallowed. *Fuck.* I knew he saw my eyes heat as he shifted and, with a twitch of his three-ringed tail, gestured me forward. As we broke the tree line, the smell of the dirt and trees filled my senses. The wind through my fur as I ran through the trees was all I focused on. Slowly, the tension released from my shoulders. Marie was right: a run was exactly what I needed.

Plus, it gave me the chance to spend some time with just Leo. I didn't mind sharing him with Marie, but I wanted some alone time with him, too.

He slowed, and we ran side by side. Occasionally, he would bump into me or flick me with his tail. We were on a rock ledge, and I slowly walked up to it, looking down at the waterfall and the large pool it fell into.

Leo clicked, and I answered, turning to follow him down the hill. Once we were in the small clearing next to the pool, I shifted and took in the way the moonlight sparkled over the pond. I inhaled the smell of the clean water, wet earth, and trees all around us, letting it flow through me.

I looked back at Leo and his tom's eyes flashed and then refracted the stars in the sky. "This is beautiful."

Shifting, he smiled at me. "It is. I mean, the scenery is great, too, I guess, but damn, the man before me is gorgeous. Completely stunning."

"Leo . . ." I couldn't help but blush.

"Seriously, the way you hold yourself and don't let anyone walk over you, just because Marie is the doctor? It's fascinating. You still command a room. Command the respect of everyone in Landow. I hear people talk, Hadrian. The pride is impressed with *both* of you."

I didn't know what to do with that compliment. Heat rose within me, though, and I tipped my head back to look up through the trees to the stars. Leo's arms wrapped around me and spread out over my stomach. We stood like that for long minutes before I leaned back into him. He softly kissed the mating spot, and my entire body flooded with electricity.

"Love . . ."

"Yeah?" His tongue swirled, and as he pulled himself closer to me, I felt just how hard he was against my ass. My hand covered his and squeezed. "This place is one of my favorite midnight getaway spots."

His words were muttered against my skin as he left a trail of kisses up my neck and then nibbled at my ear. Slowly, his hand ventured down and palmed me through my jeans. Leaning my head all the way back on his shoulder, I just took it in.

My mate was holding me, touching me. My hips moved, and when I moaned, he chuckled in my ear and kissed my neck. His other hand went up my chest, wrapped around my throat, and gripped my jaw. Turning me to face him as he took a step back, he kissed me, running his tongue along the seam of my lips. I opened for him, but he chuckled and pulled back.

Holding my full attention, he released the button on my jeans and lowered the zipper. "Strip."

My brain froze for a split second, but then I did as he said, setting my clothes off to the side. When I turned around, he had undressed and was stroking himself. My focus marked every pull and push of his movement, and I licked my lips.

"Hadrian, eyes on me."

It took considerable effort, but I slowly lifted my attention from his cock and up his muscled chest, along his neck, jaw, before finally meeting his eyes. He lifted his free hand and curled a finger in a come here motion. Taking the two steps toward him, I went to my knees before him. Submitting to Leo was a heady feeling. I swallowed as I took him in and saw the pre-cum on the tip.

"You have a choice."

I studied every ripping muscle of his as I looked up at him, waiting.

"Do you want my cock in your mouth, or do you want me to bury myself deep in your ass?"

His words tightened every muscle in my body that instantly released with desire and need. "Ass. Please, Leo."

"Love that answer." Bending down, he placed my chin between his thumb and forefinger as he kissed me softly, muttering against my lips, "Face the water on all fours."

As I did, I heard him digging in his jeans. Looking over my shoulder, I saw him set something down on the ground, but then he spread me wide. I took a deep breath and then let out a moan as I felt his tongue caressing my balls, and then move toward my ass. He circled the puckered skin there, and I was thankful I had taken the extra time in the shower this evening.

With every lick and nibble, pleasure rolled through me. Leo worked his way back down with his mouth, and as his finger pressed against me, I relaxed against him. He sucked one of my balls into his mouth as his finger worked in and out, then added another, stretching me, preparing me for him.

After a few more strokes, he released me and sat back. "This will be a little cool."

Then, he was working some lube into me. I pushed back against him as he continued, and I had to remember to breathe. "Love . . . I . . ."

"No, not yet," he commanded, and I took a really deep breath to calm myself down. "Are you mine?"

"Yes."

His free hand roamed over the fleshy parts of my ass as he continued stretching and working more lube into me.

"This ass is mine."

"Yours."

"Are you giving it to me tonight? Willingly?"

"Yes." I breathed. "Only yours. Nobody else's."

Taking more lube in his hands, he stroked himself and then ran the head of him along me. I pushed back toward him. The feel of his hands on me, loving me so tenderly, had me tingling all over.

As he lined himself up and pressed against me, I had the fleeting thought that I wouldn't be able to take all of him. I relaxed and allowed Leo in, and he pushed past the muscle. A moan came from deep within me at the feeling of Leo filling me. As he slid against every pleasure point, I had to grab the base of my cock to keep from coming immediately.

"Love." I breathed as he stretched me further. He was so much more than I had imagined. Sure, I was intimately aware of how large he was, but to have him sliding into me, stretching me . . . Hell, it was all-consuming.

"It's okay. You can take all of me, Hadrian. You wanted my cock, right?"

"Yes." I hissed as he moved slowly. "I just . . . Fuck."

"You can take it. Look at you right now. You are doing such a fucking good job, taking me." His hand ran up my spine, wrapped around my throat, and pulled me up, seating him fully within me. When I looked over my shoulder to face him, he pulled from me and pushed back in. "Look at you, taking me like the good boy you are. Fuck, you feel good."

Pleasure at his words and the feeling of him moving within me had every nerve on fire. "Yes, love. Please. Fuck me hard."

"Anything for my mate." He kissed me and then said, "Hold on tight, my Hadrian."

Then, he was gripping my throat and hip, railed into me. With every thrust, I was moaning and meeting him, the slapping of our bodies together canceling out all other sounds. Others had tried, but no male had ever made me feel euphoric. The cool breeze caressed our skin as he pounded into me, and I could feel myself getting close. This man knew exactly how to please me, how to draw out my pleasure. "Leoooo . . . ," I groaned.

"That's it, Hadrian, come for me." He thrust into me hard and fast, rolling his hips, sending wave after wave of pleasure through me. My hand pumped along my cock as we moved, my hand squeezing around the head. Leaning against me, he sucked in at the mating spot, and the pleasure that rocked through me had me releasing within seconds.

A few strokes later, Leo was pounding into me hard as he screamed my name, filling me with his cum completely before he stilled. With a breathy voice, he kissed the mating spot again and muttered, "Fuck, that was better than I imagined."

Turning and looking over my shoulder at him, I nodded. "Yeah, it was."

CHAPTER 15

MARIE

"Thank you, Ms. Jones. Please let us know if the rash spreads," Hadrian said as he walked the elderly woman out to the front porch of the clinic.

I was making a few more notes when one of our medical assistants came around the corner. "Dr. Fuller, Princess Ronni is here."

My heart started racing as I hurried down the hall in time to hear, "Sorry, Hadrian. I don't want to worry Mase yet, but—"

"It's okay, Princess Ronni. Come on inside. Let's see what's going on." I looked up to see Angelica and Hadrian helping Princess Ronni. The worried look on Hadrian's face had my heart racing. His focus dropped to her legs, and when I looked, my heart about jumped out of my chest. There was a significant amount of blood on her dress on the right side near her center, and a line of it was running down the inside of her leg.

"Dr. Fuller?"

"Please set up OR 3." I took a long, deep breath through my nose and I pulled on every ounce of professionality I had in me, as Ronni's wide eyes met mine. "Let's take a look and see what we are dealing with."

Once we had her in the bed in the OR and got her hooked up to the monitors, I looked at Angelica, whose focus was where the blood was on Ronni's dress. Hadrian touched her shoulder and jerked his head back, and she took a couple of steps toward the wall.

I grabbed a surgical gown, sterile gloves, and finished scrubbing up. Once the princess was lying back on the table, I slid her dress to her waist, where her thighs were covered in blood.

Fuck.

"Princess Ronni, first, how do you feel?"

"Starting to freak out a bit." Her breathing picked up, and she looked to Angelica with wide eyes. "To answer your question, though, I just feel off. I didn't want to be a bother, but I just want to be sure. I started bleeding on the way over here."

My gaze met Hadrian's, and he nodded and started prepping.

"Any contractions?"

She shook her head. "No. Just felt weird."

"Okay. So, as you know, you are bleeding. It means the placenta has continued to dislodge." My focus went to her eyes. Flickers of fear and then determination went through them before she nodded in understanding.

Angelica was fidgeting and her eyes were wide with worry. After prepping a few things, I turned toward her and waited to catch her attention. "We are going to move forward with the cesarean. Go tell Prince Masen that he is about to be a father, and if he is not here by the time I start operating, then he will not be allowed in this room. He will have to watch his cubs be born from the window. On your way out, hit the yellow button by the door."

"Yes, ma'am." Angelica turned, hit the button, shifted as she hit the hallway, and was off.

Ronni's attention went from the door to me and with a deep breath, she said, "Marie?"

"Yes, princess."

"No. Not princess. I am your sister right now, and I am asking for one thing."

"I'm going to cut this dress open. Sorry." I took the scissors to it, and she ignored me. "And if you are going to ask me to save the babes over you, I will smack you. We made a promise to our mate that we would do everything we could to save all three of you. So, get that thought out of your fucking head right now, Ronni."

"Hadrian?" Ronni said, turning toward him with the same plea-filled eyes we had seen on so many mothers before.

"Sorry, Ronni. You are going to have to settle for living a long, happy life with the prince and your two cubs."

"But if the choice has to be made—"

"No!" we both said firmly.

Hadrian finished prepping the equipment and grabbed two pediatric beds from the other room for the babes. I was just about ready as I asked, "You have the block?" With a nod to me, I looked to the door just as Ronni groaned, and the bleeding became heavier. Nurse Practitioner Jarrett and OR Nurse Carter came in at that moment. "Lock the door."

Jarrett locked the door, scrubbed, and I prepped. "Ready."

"Okay, princess, I need you to roll over to face me while Hadrian gives you something to block the pain."

CHAPTER 16

LEO

Masen was doing his best not to show it, but he was twitchy. He rolled his shoulders and was tapping his fingers on the table. I lifted my eyebrow at him, and he gave me a small shake of the head.

"Look, Councilman Jones, Los Padres is already in a dire situation with providing just the necessities to their pride," Morgan said just as there was a commotion outside the conference room doors.

Blinking, I recognized Angelica's voice. My gaze met Morgan's, and he looked at us questioningly. When there was a bang on the door, he stood just as we heard her screaming. "I'm here under the orders of Dr. Fuller. Let me in. I have to speak to Prince Masen, now."

We rushed to the doors as the guard said, "They are in a closed meeting, ma'am."

"Do I look like I give a fuck?" she screamed. "Prince Masen needs to get to the clinic, right now."

Morgan pulled the door open to Angelica being held back by two guards, her feet swinging in the air wildly. His growl rolled through the space, and the guards let her go as she looked at Masen. "Mase, get to the clinic. The cubs are coming."

Masen's eyes went wide, and he took off. I looked behind us to the king, who nodded and jutted his chin out for us to go.

"Meeting cancelled. We will discuss . . ." I heard him say as Angelica, Morgan, and I took off behind Masen.

We bolted out of the main chambers and into the street. Everyone moved out of the way as we rushed through Landow. Masen shifted and sped off, pulling away from us.

Angelica shifted and split through the alley to the right. A block up, we turned in the direction of the clinic. When we got there, Masen was standing off before Angelica, his power radiating through the room, roaring, "Move, Angelica. Sister or not, you will move so that I can be with Ronni."

Her muscles trembled with the command. So rarely I had seen Masen use his royal blood to command, but he *was* using it now, and I couldn't blame him. Her gaze flicked to me, and I nodded to her. She shook her head and met Masen's eyes again.

"They locked the door, Mase. Dr. Fuller said that we wouldn't be allowed in there if they had already started the operation. We can watch from the window."

I looked through the window and saw Hadrian. He looked up, and there was an apology in his eyes before he went back to work helping Marie. I took a deep breath and looked back at Masen, who was quickly becoming unglued. My gaze met Marie's, and she gave me a small nod.

Come on, baby. Do what you do best.

The door opened behind us, and a wave of power blew through the room at the single command. "Masen, stop."

Turning, I saw the only two people who were going to be able to reel Masen in. "Your Majesties."

Masen moved to the window and watched as Marie reached in, and a moment later, we could see the head of baby number one. Hadrian was there a moment later, handing her a few tools, and she did a few things that were blocked from our view before wiggling baby number one out and cutting the umbilical cord. Marie handed baby number one to Jarrett, and she went to work cleaning and checking over the cub, who after a moment, started wailing.

"You are doing great, Ronni." Hadrian's voice carried through the speaker and into the room we were in, and I saw Masen's shoulders relax. In that moment, Ronni rolled her head to face us, and Masen's hand reached up and pressed against the glass.

Marie was working on baby number two when Ronni mouthed the words, "I love you."

"I love you too, kitten."

Suddenly, alarms were going off like crazy, causing Marie and Hadrian to look at a screen just behind Ronni's head. My attention snapped to it, and I saw flashing numbers that climbed really high and others that were dropping. My focus went to Ronni and I watched as her face drained of color. The monitor on the wall continued to blare through the space as I watched numbers all over the screen plummet.

"Ronni . . . ," I whispered in horror.

Hadrian was there, working on her instantly, and Marie worked with more earnestness.

"Kitten!" Masen screamed.

The world faded and slowed to a crawl around me.

Marie was giving instructions to Hadrian.

The second baby was born, and it took longer for it to start crying. There was a bit of jostling and firm rubbing by Marie before we finally heard a wail and it was handed over to Nurse Carter.

Focusing back on Hadrian, I saw he was working on Ronni.

Our princess. My sister.

Marie was talking to Hadrian in what seemed like a different language as they worked in tandem to make sure that Ronni came back to us. Machines were blaring through the rooms, and Masen continued to freak out, his fists banging on the glass as he roared Ronni's name.

We all just stared at Ronni and watched as they worked.

It felt like a lifetime.

My whole body was frozen. My tom whimpered in the background of my mind, and the pride laws pushed and pulled at my body, urging me to do something to help her. I knew there was nothing I could do right now but watch my mates do their jobs, and it was killing me.

Masen, however, was still screaming and pounding on the window. It cracked under the pressure of the last impact as Morgan wrapped his arms around his waist and hauled him back from it. "Take a breath, Mase."

It was the queen who whipped around and stood in his face. "Masen, you need to calm down. Look at them. They are doing everything they can. When she wakes back up, she needs you calm and collected, *not* in absolute hysterics."

"She's dying," he growled. "I can feel it."

While I was scared to death that Ronni wouldn't walk out of that room, I met his growl with my own.

"Do you not have enough faith in my mates to save her?" His eyes met mine, and while there was pain and fear there, I saw the moment he dialed it all back. "My mates made a promise to me they would do everything they can for her. Do you really think they would willingly break that promise to *me*? Do you think they would let *their* princess die on that table?"

"Leo . . ." His voice was broken. "I can't lose her."

My focus went inside the room as I saw Hadrian give Marie a nod before bending down and whispering something in Ronni's ear. There was the smallest nod from her, and I relaxed. Hadrian's gaze flicked to me quickly and he gave me a wink before he looked back at Marie.

"Now, look back into that room and see that my mates have done *exactly* what they promised."

Masen looked back to where Hadrian and Marie were looking through the window. While their hands were busy working on Ronni, Marie shouted, "Ronni is fine. She just passed out for a moment. Congratulations, you have a son and a daughter."

Masen's face slowly morphed from fear to elatedness. "A son and a daughter?"

Ronni's head rolled toward us, and as she opened her eyes to look at Masen, she broke out into a smile. They held each other's attention for another long moment while Marie and Hadrian continued to work. While they cleaned her up, Jarrett and Carter continued to clean up the babies. It didn't take them too long, but Masen was pacing and antsy to get in there.

The door eventually popped open, and Jarrett stepped outside of the room and said, "Prince Masen, if you would follow me, we need to get you cleaned up so you can meet your son and daughter."

"Thank you." He followed her to another room, and then Nurse Carter wheeled the babies around to the window for us to see.

Two little bins sat on the other side of the glass panes, and Angelica, Morgan, and I pressed against it. Both swaddled in light-green blankets, one had a little dusting of dark hair all over their head, the boy, while our little girl had a small tuft just on the top.

"They're perfect," Morgan mumbled next to me.

Angelica had one hand on the glass and the other on her stomach, with her mouth moving quickly. She looked over at me and smiled brightly. "We are aunts and uncles."

"We are," I said in awe as we turned back to where the babies were. Masen came into view, and Jarrett picked them up and placed them in his arms.

Tears lined my eyes as Mase started crying, looking at them. His attention went to us in the window, and he smiled. "They are here, and Ronni is okay."

Turning, he carried our new princess and prince over to Ronni and we watched her give them each a little kiss on the head. I let out a long breath in relief. My attention went to my mates, both still working diligently on Ronni. Marie's eyes found mine, and

I saw the crinkle around her eyes as she smiled. I mouthed, "Thank you," and she nodded with a gleam in her eyes as her attention went back to Ronni.

CHAPTER 17

HADRIAN

It took a couple hours after the babies were born to get Princess Ronni fully settled and into a room where she and Prince Masen could be together. If we had been in the city, we would have taken the babes to the NICU, but we got them settled and monitored in the OR with Jarrett and Carter watching over them. They were breathing well on their own, and we were glad for the shifter abilities making that possible. Masen and Ronni had told the family that Princess Brooke Jasmine and Prince Ethan Aster would be available for the family to visit tomorrow, when Princess Ronni had more energy.

Marie had stepped back into the office to finish some paperwork, told me to head home, and assured me that she would be along soon. When I stepped into the waiting room, I was suddenly pushed against the wall, Leo's crisp scent wrapping around me and washing away today's stress. His lips crashed against mine, and I instantly opened for him. As his tongue danced with mine, my arms tightened around his waist, pulling him closer to me.

He leaned back and was breathing hard as his fingers tightened around my neck, causing my eyes to roll back in my head. "Fuck, love."

I felt the smile that graced his face against my lips, and when I opened my eyes to meet his sparkling blue ones, he just muttered, "Thank you."

"For what exactly?" I breathed.

"For you and Marie keeping your promise."

"Love, you don't have to thank us for protecting our family." There was something feral in his eyes, though, that was coated in lust. I swallowed and waited. We hadn't mated yet, and my tom was getting really cranky about it. He was all in with Leo, and neither of us could wait for the three of us to be joined.

"I know. I know, but I still feel like I have to say it." His voice hitched, and he took a slow breath. "Where is Marie?"

"Finishing her paperwork," I whispered, and he leaned back, but I rested my hand on his chest, right above his heart. "What is wrong? Your heart is thundering."

"What? It can't run to the races when the sexiest man alive is kissing and holding me?" I chuckled because it was corny but sweet at the same time. "I want to complete the mating with you and Marie. Tonight."

I stared at him, and my focus bounced between his eyes. All I saw was his love for me. I didn't see any doubts as I smiled so hard that my cheeks hurt. The door beside us opened to Marie standing there, out of breath. "Seriously?"

Leo looked between us, wrapped a hand around the back of her neck, and pulled her to him, kissing her. The way she melted against him warmed my heart. "Yes, and not just because of today. Today was just . . . you doing your jobs."

She swallowed, but I saw the heat in her eyes. "I-I . . ." Marie took a deep breath, looked back toward her office, and finally said, "I have some charting that *has* to be done same-day. I need thirty minutes before I can leave."

He kissed her again and then ordered in that voice that had my tom perking up, "Then get it done, baby, and meet us at the house. We will stop by the store and get something easy for dinner."

Marie's eyes glazed over, flashed as her queen acknowledged the order, and she licked her lips before turning back through the door.

"Baby!" She looked over her shoulder, and he crooked a finger to have her come back. She did, and her eyebrows pinched in confusion. "I know I said it earlier, but thank you for all that you two did today."

"I've already told him we were just doing our jobs."

"Still. It's one thing for you to do what you did today on some random shifter with a problematic pregnancy, but this was my sister. Your sister. Our princess." He swallowed, and I saw his eyes glaze over.

Marie reached up and cupped his cheek. "It was our honor, love."

Nodding and turning to kiss her palm, he held her gaze for a moment before I saw heat fill them again. A smile fell across his lips as he said, "Now, get what you need to done, baby. I need to claim my mates tonight."

A bright smile graced her face, and the red in her cheeks was stunning. She turned and ran back to her desk.

I kept my voice low but said, "Seeing you order her around like that is hot as hell, love."

He raised an eyebrow at me and pressed me against the wall again. His voice was all domination as he breathed against my lips. "Seeing you follow my directions last night as I fucked you was hot as hell, Hadrian. Sealing our bond tonight? That will make last night look like a teenage romp."

My tom purred at the promise. I couldn't find my words, so I just nodded.

"So." He pulled back and took my hand, pulling me through the large, empty waiting room and out the front door. "What sounds good for dinner?"

CHAPTER 18

LEO

As Marie was bent over after dinner, putting away a couple of pots, I couldn't resist smacking her luscious ass. There was a delightful moan that came from her, and when she looked up at me, I lifted an eyebrow. She stood, glancing at Hadrian, and I watched as her cheeks flushed. When her focus came back to me, Marie stepped up so there were only a couple of inches between us and looked up through her long lashes at me. Gripping her chin, I looked down at her as Hadrian came to stand beside her, wrapping his hand around my belt.

Heat filled their eyes as they stared back at me. I bit my lip as my heart raced with the magnitude of what I was about to ask them. Reaching over, I ran my hand up his arm and gripped his neck. His whimper vibrated against my palm as his eyes glazed over. "Are you willing to bind yourself to me?"

Hadrian's voice was husky as he muttered, "Nothing would make me happier."

"Marie?" I swallowed as I awaited her response.

She nodded her head as much as she could with me holding her chin but smiled. "I'd be awfully disappointed if you—"

I kissed her, stopping her from talking, sliding my hand around the back of her neck as she melted into me.

"Fuck. I am the luckiest person on the fucking planet."

"We beg to differ." Marie's smile was wide, and her bright green eyes sparkled in the kitchen lights.

Looking between them, I thought about how I wanted to claim my mates. I pulled Hadrian to me and kissed him hard. Releasing his lips, I leaned back and, to Marie, breathed, "Baby, I hope you don't mind being very full."

Her eyes heated as I turned to face her. "I can't wait."

Hadrian's finger hooked around the loop of my belt and pulled me toward the bedroom. Marie reached over and threaded her fingers with mine as we headed down the hall.

Once inside our room, I pushed Hadrian against the wall and gripped his T-shirt, ripping it from his body. His purr rumbled against me as I rolled my hips against him, my lips leaving open-mouthed kisses along his neck. My heart was pounding, and all I could think was that I finally had them. I finally had my mates. My tom sat back, agreeing and rubbing against me in want. Hadrian's fingers went to work, undoing my belt, as Marie's hands took hold of my T-shirt and lifted it over my head.

Spinning around and grinding my ass against Hadrian, I reached down, my claws extending as I tore her shirt off her. They retracted, and I ran a single finger down Marie's throat. She tipped her head back, moaning at my touch as I trailed that finger down and pinched her nipple between the lace of her bra. She gasped and sucked in her bottom lip before opening her eyes.

Hadrian slipped my jeans down, kissing down my back. I swore I heard a guttural growl come from him as I stepped out of them and he did the same. Marie's clothes were quickly removed, and she knelt before me and wrapped her hand around both of our cocks, pumping them. She leaned forward and ran her tongue around the head of mine, and I moaned as Hadrian leaned over and kissed me.

My hand slipped into her red hair and gripped. She moved off me and took Hadrian into her mouth. He stepped closer and tangled her hair and my fingers in his. Looking up at us, Marie took both of us and wrapped her lips around the bulbous heads of our cocks. Sucking and licking around them, she had us both moaning and biting our lips. She swallowed as much of us as she could before releasing me and fully swallowing Hadrian, just down to the silver piercing.

"Fuck, that's sexy as hell." I groaned as I pushed and pulled her up and down his length. He dragged his gaze to me and kissed me again with a moan.

A moment later, Marie had switched and was licking and sucking her way up and down my cock. My hips moved, and when hit the back of her throat, she adjusted and swallowed me. Holding herself there, she looked up at me and then pulsed a few times before releasing me with a pop.

Hadrian pulled her up and kissed her. "Seeing you with our mate's cock in your mouth almost made me lose it, baby."

She raised her eyebrows and wiped the spit that had spilled on her chin. "Well, I need both of you. So . . ." Marie backed up to the bed and stood on her knees. "Who is taking me where?"

Smiling, I took Hadrian's hand and threaded my fingers through his. "Oh, baby, you will be taking both of us right in that beautiful pussy of yours." She blinked, and Hadrian's hand squeezed mine. "Any objections?"

Her head moved slowly back and forth as her breathing hitched and she swallowed. I stepped up to her and cupped her cheek.

"Baby, what are you thinking?"

Her gaze shifted to Hadrian and then back to me. "I'm just wondering if I'll be able to take both of you."

"Have you ever had two at once?" I asked, my head tilting to the side.

Hadrian's voice was soft as he cupped her other cheek. "She has, but they were smaller than us while I took her ass. She was such a trooper that day."

"I loved it, but yeah, they were not nearly as big as my mates. I trust you, though."

"Just tell us if it's too much," I whispered against her lips. She nodded, and I leaned back. "Hadrian, do you want top or bottom?"

His cheeks heated as he kissed me and said, "Bottom." Then, he moved and lay down on the bed. Marie turned to face me and straddled his hips. Her eyes met mine as she lined him up, and I groaned as I watched him disappear into her glorious pussy.

Leaning forward, I latched onto her clit and licked every inch of her, working my way down until I sucked one of Hadrian's balls into my mouth. The whimper that came from him was inhuman as I released him and licked the base of his length and teased the nerves at her entrance before swiping up and flicking her clit. There was a catch of breath, and I watched as her muscles tensed and relaxed at the movement.

"Baby." I waited until she lifted her head to look at me. When her gaze met mine, I slid two fingers in along Hadrian's cock, watched as her eyes glazed over, and smiled at the moan Hadrian made under her. "You ready for both of us?" I pulled my fingers toward me, stretching her a little more to prepare her for us both.

"Yes, Leo. Please."

Stroking myself as I stepped forward, I ran my fingers along Hadrian's legs, relishing the twitch of muscles. Marie rolled against him, and my attention went right to where they were joined. My gaze traveled up her body to where her head leaned back, eyes closed in pleasure. I watched as she lifted and fell on him.

I ran the head of me along Hadrian, and he brought Marie down so he was fully sheathed within her. Pressing the head of me in, I paused as her mouth opened into an euphoric O.

"Look at me."

Her eyes opened, her gaze snapping to mine as I slid in along Hadrian into her warmth. She was tight, but as I moved deeper into her, our queen accommodated us both.

Hadrian and Marie. My mates.

She bit her lower lip, and when I looked over her shoulder, I could see Hadrian with his head thrown back in bliss.

"Look at you, baby, taking both of us." I slowly dragged out of her and pushed back in. Hadrian's cock was smooth as silk along me, and I felt the heat of them through my whole body. I was with my mates. These two would be all I would ever need.

As long as I had them, I would be whole. I would be complete.

My heart swelled as Hadrian and I moved with each other inside of our queen. The sound of our bodies working as one, the moans and groans of my mates filling the space was all music to my ears. Hadrian twitched and grew against me as Marie tightened around us both.

"I am yours." I groaned, and they responded with their own, "Yours."

"Fuck," Marie groaned. My gums tingled as I watched them in their bliss. "Yes."

Her whole body shook with her orgasm as she squeezed around me and Hadrian. My fangs snapped down and I struck her shoulder, piercing the skin. As soon as her blood hit my lips, I felt the world spin and her fangs strike my shoulder. The universe burst through my chest as we released each other. Marie moved to the side, and Hadrian's fangs lowered and dug into my shoulder right next to where Marie had marked me.

"Fuck yes!" I moaned as I marked him as mine, and I felt his cock twitch with the force of his release. My lips wrapped around the spot where my fangs struck, and I licked along the one Marie had left on him. As their souls took residence with mine, my heart beat loud in my ears and that fiery warmth I first felt when meeting them spread through my body. With the last thump, my release joined theirs.

Kneeling there panting and spent, I leaned back, feeling our combined releases slide from her. My legs were wobbly as I looked at them, their eyes shining back with love.

"Hadrian." I shifted my gaze to Marie. "Marie, I love you both."

Marie's eyes filled with tears, her mouth opening and closing as Hadrian whispered, "I love you, too."

"You okay, baby?"

"Why wouldn't I be?"

I huffed a laugh. "You were worried you wouldn't be able to take us both."

Kissing me, she smiled. "That was the most amazing thing I've done in my life. I will forever cherish this memory."

Hadrian kissed her temple with a smile on his lips. Slowly, I pulled from her and ordered, "Stay here. I'll get us cleaned up."

CHAPTER 19

MARIE

A knock sounded on the front door, and I went to tell whoever it was that Leo had stepped out for a minute. Only, when I opened it, Doc stood there.

"Well, *you* look better." I smiled at them.

A bright smile crossed their lips as they shook their head. "Is Hadrian home? I'd like to talk to you both if you have a few minutes."

"Um, yeah, come on in." I opened the door wider and hollered, "Hadrian! Doc is here to talk to us."

He came out of the laundry room and shut the door behind him. "Hi, Doc. Everything alright?"

"Yes, sir. Just wanted to talk to you and Dr. Fuller." They went and sat on the chair that was opposite the couch and leaned forward on their knees. "I understand you mated with Leo a few days ago."

A large smile crossed my face. "We did."

"And you are both planning on staying here?" They lifted an eyebrow in question.

I looked to Hadrian, whose brows furrowed at Doc. "Yes. We are. We have a meeting with the king tomorrow to work out logistics."

Doc chuckled. "Yeah, he pushed that meeting from today, didn't he?"

Now I narrowed my eyes at the older kismot across from me. "Doc, what are you getting at?"

"I have already talked to King Harsu. If you accept, the clinic will be transferred into your name and list you as head physician."

I blinked and felt my mouth drop open. Hadrian's hand took mine and squeezed. "I'm sorry, what?"

They shook their head. "I'm offering you the clinic as head physician. I want to retire soon anyway. We can transition things over slowly, if you want. Jarrett can cover when you and Hadrian need to help someone. King Harsu isn't standing in the way of that."

I turned to look at Hadrian again, and his eyes met mine. I swallowed and waited for him to say something. He opened his mouth, but then the front door opened and Leo walked in. He stopped a few steps in and looked at the three of us sitting there.

"Doc." Leo nodded in greeting and then looked at us, his brows pinching together in question. "Everything okay?"

I reached my free hand out toward Leo, and he came and took it, threading his fingers through mine. He brought our joined hands up to his lips and kissed them. "Yeah, umm . . ."

Doc chuckled and leaned back in the chair. "I've already talked to the king. The clinic is hers."

"That isn't what you just said. You said if I accepted!" I exclaimed.

Doc looked at me and shrugged. "Well, do you want it?"

Confusion hit me, and I looked at the floor. My boys tightened their grips on my hands, and when I turned to each of them, I knew they were leaving it up to me to decide. I faced Doc, letting out a long breath. I knew I'd be giving up my practice in Eureka, but Hadrian and I had been too busy to think of much else, other than to see if the king would allow us to stay on and still help other shifters throughout the state. "Yeah. I'd be honored."

"Good, because the pride loves you two. I've had a lot of people come and say that they felt like they were listened to and well taken care of while I've been down." They let out a small cough, cleared their throat, and smiled. "There is one condition."

"I'm listening." My heart was pounding in my chest.

Their chin lifted as they looked at Leo and then me. "Make Leo happy for the rest of your lives."

Hadrian let out a chuckle. "That is the easiest condition I think you could have given her."

"Agreed." Leo huffed a laugh beside me. "Them walking into this town and into Ronni's bedroom is the best thing that has ever happened to me." He leaned over, kissed my temple, took his finger, and turned me by my chin to have me look at him. "This is what you want? You are willing to be responsible for the health and wellness of the entire pride? I don't want you to agree to this just because of me. You can stay on as a doctor. Hadrian too."

"I have a practice up north. I know how to run a clinic. The location is the only thing that has changed. Plus, I get to keep the pride safe, albeit differently than you do, but I get to help my community."

He looked behind me to Hadrian, and I felt him squeeze my hand. I'm assuming he gave Leo the answer he needed because Leo leaned down and kissed me softly before whispering, "Okay."

"I'll ask King Harsu to have all the paperwork ready for your meeting with him."

"Thank you, Doc," I said as we stood and then shook their hand. "Thank you for trusting me."

CHAPTER 20

LEO

THREE WEEKS LATER

We'd finished dinner, and as we settled on the couch, Ronni handed me a baby bottle. I adjusted Princess Brooke in my arm, where she sighed when I gave it to her. It was hard to believe that they were already three weeks old.

"Already has Uncle Leo wrapped around her thumb." Masen smirked as he gave Prince Ethan his.

"Well, when she cries in your arms and I'm the only one to calm her, then yes. Yes, she does." I looked down at the little button nose on her face as she sucked on the bottle. Hadrian sat down next to me, wrapping his arm around my back on the couch and brushing the little smattering of dark hair on the top of her head.

It was Marie, though, who I looked at, and the tears in her eyes surprised me. "Baby, what's wrong?"

She sniffed and wiped at the tear that escaped. "Nothing. I just can't wait for the day we are holding our own."

I smiled at her because she and I had talked about it earlier that morning while Hadrian was making breakfast. We both knew that Hadrian was all in, but I was the one that initially wanted to hold off. Now, I was totally on board. I held her gaze but noticed how everyone else in the room went still. Hadrian's hand caressed my neck as he said, "Baby, you should be going into heat in a month. Are you . . ." He looked at me, and I smiled at him before looking back at Marie. "Do you want to try right away?"

Her head bobbed, and Angelica instantly wrapped her up in a hug. "Well, all of us will have our kids about the same age."

Masen turned to face her. "What?"

Morgan shifted to stand next to Angelica and pulled her close. Marie's eyes went down to the floor, and a small smile crossed her lips. "Marie verified it this morning for us. We are pregnant."

The room erupted into cheers as much as we could without disturbing Brooke and Ethan.

Once everyone settled down, I burped Brooke, and she instantly went into a coma in my arms, her little finger wrapped around mine. I smiled at her, kissed her little head, and just held her. Hadrian chuckled next to me before he kissed my temple as we sat around, just chatting.

Masen and Ronni were more than happy to let us hold the babies. They were exhausted. Plus, Marie kept getting after Ronni for how much she was doing.

"Everything seems so easy with you three," Morgan said, pulling Angelica in close.

Hadrian looked at me, and I shook my head, smiling. "What do you mean *easy*?"

"Well, there was no major issue."

Marie's eyes narrowed, as if my mates were thoroughly confused. Saving them from having to go through twenty questions, I told them, "With Morgan and Angelica, we basically had to run away with her."

"What?" they asked in unison.

Angelica laughed. "Yeah, my dad is Lynis McCullen."

"No." Marie's eyes were wide. "He is not."

She nodded her head. "He is. Tried to sell me off in his trafficking ring. Twice. Hell, I didn't even know I was kismot until after I was with Morgan and we mated. Another story, another time. He got what was coming to him, though."

"Then there was Ronni," I said softly, my heart breaking at all Mase and Ronni had had to endure.

"Doc said that there was severe trauma, and well, I saw the evidence of that, but how?" Marie asked.

I took her hand in mine and laced my fingers with hers. "The short story is that she was the Los Padres Pride's undesirable for most of her life. The princes were not kind to her, and one had an unhealthy obsession with her. He was disposed of, but . . ."

My eyes met Morgan's, and he let out a long breath. "We aren't done with the Los Padres Pride just yet. The other prince now seems to want to create issues. We will deal with him."

Hadrian took hold of my thigh and squeezed it. When I looked at him, he simply asked, "Is this one of those situations where you can't tell us?" I nodded. "You'll stay safe, though, right?"

I smiled. "I'll always do everything within my power to make my way back to you two."

"That isn't what I asked."

"It isn't, but that is the one promise I can't make. I will be put in harm's way. I will get hurt, and I'll hope that my mates won't be too pissed off at me to put me back together again. This is part of being one of the hands to the Crown Prince of the Venanta Wilderness Pride. Hadrian, Marie, I love you with everything that I am, but I can't make that promise to you."

They nodded and said, "We love you too."

Hadrian took my hand and brought it to his lips. "Which is why we need you to come home. We expect to have a long, fulfilling life with our mate."

BOOKS ALSO BY KIMBERLY M. RINGER

The Ashstrike Sanctorum Series

The Astral's Bonded

The Exorci's Touch

My Kismot Savior

The Kismot's Undesirable

The Therugi's Shiver

The Five Angels Trilogy

The Five Angels

The Ash'bani

The Helena Crystal

A Five Angels Novel

Duchess' Crown

Duchess' Throne

Other Books

Ashes and Flame

Weekend Series

Weekend with Rylie

Weekend with Malcom

Weekend with Desiree

Weekend with Bethany

THE ASHSTRIKE SANCTORUM: CREATION STORY

When the Dark Witches of Moesia go rogue, and start creating immortals, will the paranormal creatures allow the new beings to live, or will they be out to destroy them? They have tasked Benjamin, an Ovexa, with finding three of these immortals to be interrogated to determine if they can be trusted to keep the paranormal world a secret from the humans.

Jorgen Hegland has found himself newly made but quickly learns being an immortal isn't worth it. When Benjamin finds him and demands he meet with the other creatures of the world, he agrees, but it isn't until he finds his mate, that he decides he will fight for his right to live.

The Astral's Bonded
The Ashstrike Sanctorum:
Book 1
Even Alphas have to answer to someone.

It was supposed to be a simple assignment. Astral Jade Romero was supposed to fix the werewolf problem at the Porter Ranch.

Only there was a problem, she hadn't prepared herself for, the human foreman Kolton Webster. He occupied all her thoughts and sucked her in like she never had been before.

When the wolves attack and Jade is injured will it be Kolton or the wolves that destroy her?

THE EXORCI'S TOUCH
THE ASHSTRIKE SANCTORUM:
BOOK 2

WHAT DO YOU DO WHEN YOUR ASSIGNMENT
DOESN'T DIE.

Exorci Jesse Westbrook can't touch anyone with his bare skin. If he does, they die. Such is the curse of an Exorci, the executioners for the Ashstrike Sanctorum.

His job is as simple and complicated as that. Receive the name and location of the person, and with a simple touch, the extermination is complete.

Jesse's life isn't all death and destruction. He has Maddie Taylor. The woman is his forever, but he's never dared to truly touch her. When her brother dies, her life spirals out of control, to the point she pushes Jesse from her life. Now... Now she's his next assignment.

141

<u>MY KISMOT SAVIOR</u>
<u>THE ASHSTRIKE SANCTORUM:</u>
<u>BOOK 2.5</u>

Angelica's life has been nothing but hiding from her parents and trying to make ends meet. It's been hard, but worth the freedom it afforded her from her family.

Morgan would have never guessed he would have found his queen just walking down the streets of Carmel, California, but there she was, arguing with the most despicable of women.

When Morgan intervenes, chaos ensues and Angelica and Morgan's secrets come to light quickly. Only Angelica seems to have one more...

<u>THE KISMOT'S UNDESIRABLE</u>
<u>THE ASHSTRIKE SANCTORUM:</u>
<u>BOOK 3</u>

Masen Cartwell was the son to the pride's king. It was his responsibility to ratify the treaty by marrying the Los Padres pride's undesirable, Veronica Aktins. There is something about her though. Something that pulls at his protective instincts and calls to his tom.

Ronni was the daughter of traders to her pride, an outcast, the Undesirable. Used and assaulted by the princes, the King has demanded that she marry the rival pride's prince and kill the Ventana Prides ruling family. Only, when she meets Prince Masen, his possessiveness over her and the adoration he showers her with sings to her heart.

When Prince Edwin steals Ronni, Masen will do anything to get her back. He had promised to protect her and keep her safe from her old pride.

Masen Cartwell won't let anything happen to what is his, and will stop at nothing to have his Queen back.

MY KISMOT'S BELOVEDS

<u>THE THERUGI'S SHIVER</u>
<u>THE ASHSTRIKE SANCTORUM:</u>
<u>BOOK 4</u>

<u>COMING 2024</u>